SOUL JACKER

SOUL JACKER 1

by Michael John Grist

Cover art by Jozef

Thank you for supporting my work.

ISBN: 9781799014058

THE COMPLETE **SOUL JACKER** TRILOGY

Soul Jacker (Book 1)

Soul Breaker (Book 2)

Soul Killer (Book 3)

See a full glossary of terms at the back of the book.

For SY

CONTENTS

RITRY GOLIGH

1. SOUL JACKER

The needle enters Mei-An's eye socket smoothly, nestling beside her artificially whitened eyeball and passing back into her brain. She barely flinches, though I know it's uncomfortable as hell.

If not for the hunted look on her face she'd be remarkably pretty; a late twenties meta-Asiat with deep black hair and face-framing bangs to die for. Dressed in a strawberry-red gho that clings to the curves of her body, she stands out against the jack-room's muted gray walls like an aneurysm.

And she's terrified.

I offer my best calming smile and steadily depress the syringe plunger, injecting the silvery engram fluid into her head; a bespoke memory patch of language and vocational skills, enough to build a new identity beyond the wall. I draw the needle gently out then lean back, giving her time to blink away the discomfort.

"How do you feel?" I ask.

"It hurts," she says, in the clipped tones of a Calico girl. As her mouth opens I see the black tattoo on her tongue: DZ, the brand-mark of Don Zachary, brutal mob boss of the Skulks. "Like there's an ice tsunami in my head."

I nod and watch her, sitting there on the input tray of the EMR. She's too young to remember the big waves, when they carried the last dregs of Arctic ice crashing against Calico's tsunami wall. Late twenties and maybe ten years my junior, but clearly no innocent. You don't get Don Zachary's brand and stay innocent for long.

A silvery tear beads from her darting eye and I dab it away with a surgical cloth. "Let them settle for a few moments," I say, "then we'll jack in."

As I turn to go, she reaches out and takes my hand in her cold, hard fingers. "He may come looking for me."

I smile. Of course I know that. By all accounts Don Zachary's a bastard. "Just try to be calm."

I leave her, exiting the barren gray jack-room to stand in the polished steel corridor outside, alongside my assistant Carrolla. He's tall and shaven-headed, with features just shy of model-worthy. I think he must have had marine training, though he never fought in the Arctic War.

He raises an eyebrow, and I know what he's thinking. It was a calm night until Mei-An came in: a couple of drunks asking for transient joy jacks, a freighterman looking to erase a bad trip, followed by the prospect of hitting the bars soon, and now this? We're tampering with Don Zachary's property, and that puts the crosshairs squarely on us.

"She wants out," I say, "we can do that much."

Carrolla grunts. "I heard the Don crucified the last guy who crossed him. Actually nailed him to the damn tsunami wall and left him to rot. Nobody came to help. Nobody took him down. Does that sound like a good time to you, Rit?"

I shrug. There are no shortage of legends about the Don. "I'm not turning her away."

"You damn well should."

"Should I?" I look at him. "You saw the breaks. Her cheekbones are a work of art, how many times they've been surgically reset. We let her go now, she's dead. You may as well go drown her in the ocean yourself; it'd be a kinder way to die."

"She made her bed," Carrolla protests, "let her lie in it alone."

I just keep looking at him. He's a good guy, he has my back in a pinch, but he's not ruthless enough for this, though he thinks he is. Let one innocent die and it'll break him in ways he doesn't yet understand. The War made criminals of us all.

"I can't," I say.

Carrolla stares at me and I stare back, equally stubborn. So this is our impasse, where I always draw the line. I don't live for much, and I buckle to the Don when I have to, but I won't stand in the way of someone who just wants to survive.

"Don-goddamned-Zachary," Carrolla mutters eventually under his breath, giving in. "He'll pull your face right off."

I let that pass unremarked, and we stand quietly for a moment longer. In Mei-An's brain the engram will be spreading, making connections to her existing Soul; all the unique combinations of memory, experience, emotion and chemicals that make her who she is. The engram will rewrite portions of that architecture as it teaches language and skills to help her find work. It could be a passport to a new life away from the fleshpits of the Don.

I'm helping her, I think.

"I need you tight on me for this," I say into the quiet. "It's a deeper jack than usual."

Carrolla nods sharply, like a marine. He's got discipline, I'll give him that.

After a few minutes we head back into the jack-room together. Mei-An is sitting there like a dab of milk on the EMR machine's input tray, shivering slightly. The machine's old and blocky lines don't match her at all; this child of Calico's privilege, genetically designed within an inch of her life.

Carrolla tosses her a lazy smile then takes up position at the control panel. I sit on the stool in front of Mei-An and look into her wide, hunted eyes. I offer my hand and she takes it. It's good to get the skinship started in small ways, to start our systems aligning.

"There are serious risks to your Soul," I say, for the second time since she came in. I like to be certain. "Potential damage to your memory, to your wits, to your personality. I'm good at what I do but there's always a risk. I need to hear you say you're sure."

She nods swiftly. "I'm sure. I don't have a choice."

I nod. Who amongst us does? "Lie down on your side, facing me."

She does. I climb onto the tray and lie beside her.

"It'll be fine," I say. "Carrolla."

Carrolla pushes the button to fire up the EMR; Electro-Magnetic Resonance imager. Once a piece of medical equipment designed for mapping the brain, to detect cancer, tumors and other abnormalities before they manifested outward, the EMR is now the primary tool of the Soul Jacker. Essentially an elephant-sized donut of metal and plastic tipped on its side, it contains powerful imaging electromagnets that whir within the ring, focused on the tray inside the donut hole, where the Soul Jacker and his patient lie together.

I squeeze Mei-An's hand as the electromagnets start to rev and thump, building a soupy kind of static between us, like the thickness in the air before a storm.

thump thump

thump thump

The sound grows louder and the input tray jerks into motion, drawing us into the machine's hollow heart. Like passing through the drumbeat curtain of a waterfall, the electrostatic pummels us as we slide in, until we are surrounded by the EMR's off-white bulk. The thumping of the magnets becomes thunderous and tides of electromagnetism wash out to fill the spaces between us with a cold, fluid medium. It takes years to learn how to navigate this flow, years more to jack a mind across it, but to actually jack and rewrite a Soul?

You have to be crazy.

I narrow my eyes and defocus my mind, pulling out of my own Soul and reaching out to navigate the flow between us. Dimly at first, half with my eyes and half with my mind, I glimpse the outline of Mei-An's unique Soul transposed atop her face in a hazy heatmap. Her fears, joys, memories and dreams of a better future light up bright like interweaving passageways in an endlessly overlapping maze.

I push further out, building an invisible bridge of resonance between us with my force of will alone. Across this bridge I'll pass into the outer reaches of her mind, to the spot where I injected the silvery engram. I can feel that the area's inflamed, as expected with any injection, but that's not all.

There are gnaw marks at the engram's edge, and a steady creeping corruption setting. That's unusual; too fast, too unlikely, but it can only mean-

"Shit!"

Carrolla's shout echoes tinnily through the electrostatic medium, followed by a red flash splashing down like blood in the water. Next I feel it, and I have to tamp down the inclination to panic because this jack just got real.

The Lag is here.

The Lag is the brain's natural mental immunity, present in every living mind, its sole purpose to repel any invasive presence. Here in this outer ocean of thought it comes like a goddamn shark, a great metaphysical gray beast ready to savage anything that comes close.

It's too fast. It sees me and rears back from its feeding ground at the engram before I can hide, coming both barrels right for me and ready to kill.

"Her cells are starting to cook!" Carrolla calls from far away. "Her whole brain's swelling up. Get out of there, Rit!"

I can't though, not with the engram still inside her like bloody chum to the Lag. If I don't do something fast it'll bite half her Soul away just to get the foreign matter out, and she'll come out deranged. I'm not doing that again.

"Look at me, Mei-An," I say, gazing into her wide, terrified eyes through the waves even as the extended part of me darts to evade the Lag's massive jaws. I can only do this for moments. "Look into my eyes, that's it."

She tries to nod but now she's losing motor control, making the movement uneven and jerky.

"Stay calm," I tell her, "try not to fight," then I crank the wavelength of my thoughts all the way down to match hers, initiating an invasive jack.

A rush of thought-data pummels me at once; hard bubbles rising through the magnetic flow that represent the inputs and outputs of billions of individual brain cells. I swim roughly against the barrage, able only to see the pattern of her mounting panic. Her whole system is in emergency mode and now there's only one hope: get to the core.

A second flood of thoughts buffet me like the Arctic Ocean in tsunami as her stress levels spike, the cell firing rate shoots up, and the engram area flips belly up as unconsciousness dawns…

"Damn it, Rit, she's slipping," Carrolla calls faintly from above.

I jack deeper still, down into the root and branch systems of her brain's architecture, blasting by organic structures like thick tufts of kelp, so deep I lose my grip on the world above and the sense of my own body flits away. I pass beyond the confines of brain cells and structure, through the outer crust and into the internal realm where the real world is forgotten and my mind truly meets hers.

The Molten Core.

At once lava blooms around me, the burning red and orange fire of the living mind. This is her consciousness, where she thinks, and here I am most certainly an invader, suspended like a sinking body in a churning magma tide. It is bright and chaotic with the violent churning of her thoughts.

I peer through the boiling heat. Nearby the Lag is closing in. This deep in it has transformed into a kind of worm, massive and fleshy, able to burrow through blazing lava with ease. I am powerless before it, battered and buffeted by fiery tidal flows, but I'm also the only thing that can save Mei-An's Soul.

Everything is to play for now.

I give the command and my sublavic ship forms around me, the Bathyscaphe, a submersible built for jacking through lava in the

Molten Core, as it has a thousand times before, hulled with three layers of heat-proof brick cladding. Within its belly my seven crew members burn into existence like clay pots forged in a kiln, and my consciousness splits evenly across them. As captain I send each part of myself to their posts throughout the ship: at the engines, manning the periscope, setting a course for Mei-An's Solid Core.

The engine-screw churns the ship forward, driving us into bubbles of memory that burst over the periscope and leave behind hints of who this girl is. In one I glimpse her slinging back Arctic gin in an off-wall dive bar beside a guy with a sternum piercing. In others she makes her first tentative forays across the tsunami wall and into the neon Skulks of proto-Calico, falling into company with smugglers, shits, and the children of the Don. One in particular stands out as he punches her in the face, a guy with a blunt nose and blank gray eyes. I know him but can't place the name.

The Lag snaps after me with ravenous jaws, and I launch a few sacrificial pieces of my own Soul as torpedoes to slake its hunger: the memory of my walk through the park that morning, the taste of the juice-box Carrolla brought in for me, Arcloberry, one of the newest strains out of the pack-ice. I won't miss them too much, and for the moment the Lag is distracted. It's just a hungry worm, after all, and every bit of Soul is good for food.

My sublavic ship powers ahead with the Lag chasing behind, until in moments I hear the dark boundary line of the Solid Core coming near through sonar, a heartbeat spreading through the magma with a steady-

thump thump

thump thump

-that is utterly unique, and key to deciphering Mei-An's burning mental architecture: the pattern of her mother's pulse.

The mother's pulse is the first memory formed in the infant brain, a fingerprint of the mother's heart that molds the mind like soft clay. It is the foundation all brains are built upon, with uniquely healing properties, stored in the heart of the Solid Core.

No one has ever entered a Solid Core and lived. The risks that far inside are massive, where the Lag is god and all the pathways are an endlessly shifting labyrinth. I couldn't get in if I tried, but thankfully I don't need to; I'm close enough now to tap the pulse like a keg.

Tuning forks punch out through the ship's brick cladding and capture the pattern as it resonates through the magma. The forks melt in seconds but I get what I've come for, then turn the ship around and amplify the pulse outward by vibrating the hull. The Lag instantly quiets under this gentle lullaby from the womb, and I propel my ship away from its huge body with the pulse rippling out around me, bathing Mei-An's mind with this healing balm like a key slotting into a lock.

It works, and I feel her stress levels calming through the flow of lava. I push my consciousness a few layers deeper, all the way into the realm of my ship's conning tower, into the mind of the captain standing at the periscope. Through the periscope lens I see more thoughts popping ahead; glimpses of her drugged-up latter days in the company of her blunt-nosed boyfriend. I recognize him now, one of the Don's sons who comes around sometimes to take his father's tax. He's an abusive shit who methodically beats the will out of her. The memories are calmer now, as the panic of the Lag's immune rejection stills.

thump thump, thump thump

The Lag is still out there though, tracking me sleepily through the lava. I'm still an invader, and the job isn't over. If I don't do something it will eventually scrub the engram, so I head to the tail end of the optic nerve and massage the pulse around the engram's edge, guiding it by the nose like I would a kelp-tilling shark. The pulse cools the inflamed cells and pets the Lag on the head like a trusty old dog.

I sigh with metaphoric relief.

"Can I have my Arcloberry juice box back?" I ask the Lag, a wordless information request through the magma. I remember the memory exists because I only gave the emotional content, not the frame, but the Lag is mute on its refund policy.

"My walk through the park then?" I press. "Come on, don't short me."

It bares its lipless, fleshy teeth. Fair enough, I've lost far more than this in the past, and at least I still have the frame. Nothing earth-shattering happened on my way through the park anyway. Did it?

Dammit. I pull outward, and my mind and the sublavic ship merge back into one as my thoughts suck free of Mei-An's Molten Core. I rush back through the bubbling outer soup of data as my consciousness disengages, until I'm fully back in my own head and panting hard, lying in the decelerating thump thump of the EMR machine.

Mei-An is lying in front of me, her eyes now closed and breathing deeply. The job is done.

2. MEI-AN

The tray engages and we slide out of the hollow EMR machine together, into the plain gray of the jack-room. It's painted gray for just this moment, to avoid any confusing stimulus to a disoriented brain.

"Strong work, Ritry," Carrolla says, slapping me on the back.

It takes a moment to associate his words and his movement with the impact on my back. He knows this and keeps patting until some rudimentary synchronization takes places.

I roll away from Mei-An and look up at Carrolla. He reminds me so much of someone I used to know.

"Fine work, really excellent," he says, words more to key me back to my body and sense than for anything else, "and you bedded it in too. How was the Lag?"

I slide my legs woozily off the EMR-tray and sit up with my back to Mei-An. She'll need a few hours of medicated sleep for her mind to fully settle.

"Not bad," I say. My tongue feels as thick as a wodge of dry seaweed in my mouth. Carrolla hands me a glass of water and helps me sip it. Better. "Have you got any more of those Arcloberry juice boxes though?"

He frowns. "You sacrificed the juice? Dammit, Rit. What's wrong with water, do you not have enough memories of drinking that?"

"It came to mind."

He laughs. "I heard they've got vodka mixes out at the Skulk-end, some new seed-blend. We'll hit it later. Now let's get you to recovery."

He helps me up and together we hobble out of the gray jack-room and down the polished corridor, to the glass-walled outlook space at the building's edge. Here there's a massage chair with a cerebro-sonic bath, overlooking the green-gray Arctic waves off the edge of our floating Skulk.

I settle in the chair, looking out at the gray sky and level sweep of empty ocean. Beyond the glass the Arctic spreads north into endless nothingness, into spaces where there used to be ice.

"Switch on your favorite music," Carrolla says, guiding my head into the sonic bath-well in the chair's head. He makes a good nurse, better than he'd ever have been as a marine. That's a small mercy. "You'll be up in time to party, unless Don Zachary comes for you first."

I snort, but already I'm fading as the sonic bath takes hold with a pattern of its own, attempting to mimic the sound of my mother's pulse and put me into the same womb-like state I used for Mei-An.

It's a poor imitation for most, but works well for me, since I never had a mother and the pulse I grew up to was the seven-tone chime of an artificial machine womb. In a few hours I'll wake up feeling better, and so will Mei-An. We'll probably have sex, part of the contract for those who need a little extra context to frame the re-structuring of their Soul, and that is not an entirely unpleasant notion. I drift off thinking of the War, and the few good times I can still remember.

I rouse hours later with Carrolla's steady hand on my shoulder, odd memories flitting up from the remnants of the bath; who I am and what I've done.

"You're up for it?" he asks, as he lowers the thrum of the sonic bath. "We can always dose her a bit longer if you need more time."

I blink, looking out of the window to the dark water. Still night.

"I'll do it," I say, patting Carrolla's hand. "Give me a minute."

"No problem. She's in recovery."

His footsteps clank away, and I'm left looking out of the glass again, waiting as my mind gets itself together. It's all darkness beyond, waves lapping against the Skulk's quays, but for a few buoy lights on the kelp-farms and the faint lights of ships out in the distance. All so fragile and tenuous, like newly grown strands of coral.

I get up.

Mei-An is waiting for me in the recovery room, overlooking another open swathe of gray ocean. She smiles when I come in.

"Alsh bevral I ferraqu," she says. "Kalin Very."

I nod, because she's speaking Afri-Jarvanese, one of the languages in the engram I injected. "Very good. Do you know what it means?"

"Not really. Just a feeling."

"You said good morning and wished me well. I suppose it'll be morning soon enough."

She brushes a strand of dark hair from her face. For a long moment she looks at me, sizing me up and down. It's not an unfamiliar sensation, and not entirely uncomfortable. Soul Jackers have always used sex as a balm; the fastest, safest way to bed in an engram. Back in the War, working with men and women who'd constantly needed the trauma of close-quarters combat excised, I hardly breathed between jacks and the rush of sex that followed.

"Carrolla said it'll make me feel better," she says at last.

"How do you feel now?"

"Bad. Nauseous. Like I'm not myself."

"Then it will," I say. "Or we can sit here and talk through the night, holding hands. Both will do the same."

"I don't want to talk. I don't have the time. But you don't mind?"

"It's my job." I smile, which always helps.

She raises an eyebrow, clipped like a silkworm, and walks over to me. Each step is measured, a careful gait she surely learned at one of Calico's schools of manners. She's plainly from the Calico Reach, the uppermost crust of the wealthy across the tsunami wall.

"I remember what you did," she says, taking my hand. "In the War."

Her hand is soft, small like all the Reach girls, modified to be that way. I know now why she first came out here to the Skulks; seeking adventure. She's a tourist who got pulled down into the mire, and now she wants to be free. Of course she knows something about me too, some piece of my marine life glimpsed through the EMR. This is why the post-jack physical contact is so important; to add context to knowledge that would otherwise be corrosively unsupported, helping the memory engram sprout roots in her Soul.

"Don't think about that," I say. "Come on, let's go."

Hand in hand we exit the jack-site. Carrolla gives us a nod from the reception.

Outside the air is thick with salt and rot from the off-Skulk kelp farms. Stars glimmer faintly through Calico's polluted glow. A desultory alley winds down to a nondescript dock on the left, flocked with nesting crulls, genetic half-breed of gulls and crows, and a shark-tiller's coracle. The dirty gray Arctic Ocean laps steadily at the dock's barnacle-crusted plastic flotation barrels, as dark and rhythmic as sex.

On the right the alley leads up to the tsunami wall through a gauntlet of cheap pink and purple neon, signs glowing off the Skulk's three B's; brothels, bars, and barrios. Each is lit in their own lurid fuzz like a row of hungry divas lusting for applause.

Mei-An looks at me. I know she's used to finer things; life inside Don Zachary's compound, and before that Calico itself. "How can you live here?" she asks.

"How could you?" I answer.

In places the neon is interrupted by dark gulches of shadow, lean-to escarpments and scaffolded construction projects, squat boat-holds and opium dens built out of rotten-hulled boats, much of it flotsam salvaged from the last tsunami. My jack-site doesn't look out of place here, about as equally squalid and dingy as the rest. It even has its own neon sign, chosen by Carrolla, though it's gray like brain matter and only says 'Souls Jacked!' I'm not sure if that's a joke or not, but it seems to amuse him.

With her small hot hand in mine, we head up the alley. Underfoot the Skulk fabric shifts, as the flotation barrels it rests upon flex with our weight. Ahead of us, rising above the crock-pot chimneys and uneven lines of the Skulk, stands the implacable off-white shank of Calico's tsunami wall.

It's vast, of course, as big as any dam in the pre-War days, enough to stop the fifty-foot tsunamis that churn up from quakes in the Arctic fault lines. It's been over ten years since the last big one, and we've been due another for as long as I've been here.

We're all living on borrowed time.

"You don't belong here," says Mei-An, catching me looking up at it. "You belong on the other side, in Calico. You paid your dues in the War."

"I paid enough to stay wherever I want."

She doesn't say any more, and I'm glad of it. I wouldn't want to fall out over this, not when the job is still unfinished, nor do I want to learn any more of her life with the Don's son. I have enough life histories weighing me down already.

The massage boys, whores and touts leave us alone as we pass by their neon dens, each a cave to forbidden pleasure. Some give me a wink. These are the people I drink with most nights, after the Mei-Ans are long gone to whatever life my engrams build for them.

"You must like it here," she says, as we turn off the alley and into one of the blue tarp parks. The resident homeless man, once a marine I think, shouts out something as we pass by. A few stunted trees reach upward toward neon from soil-pods dropped amongst the barrels, branching like brain cells. I imagine messages passing between their roots, electronic charges popping on-off, on-off, as the trees build the seeds that will outlive them by far. We skirt the sunken pond, where rainwater trapped in the blue plastic sheeting sags, and I wonder how I can best stem her curiosity in the fewest words.

"You know about the Lag," I say.

She nods by my side, clutching my arm more tightly now. I don't blame her, it's dark here in the Skulk-slums where the sex workers and ex-bountymen go to burrow in and ride out the daylight like vampiric worms under a rock.

"The thing in your brain that protects you by eating invaders. You know sometimes the Lag turns on itself, on its own home? People get old and they forget; it means the Lag got old too, it couldn't recognize the things it was supposed to protect. You end up with large empty expanses of memory, blank canvases where nothing more lasting can take root than what you had for dinner that night."

I pause for breath and we cross a section of sparse yellow grass. "It's like that. This whole place is a Lagged zone, a doldrums in space that doesn't mean anything to anyone. You can do anything you want out here and none of it matters, because none of it's going to last."

"And that's what you want," she says.

I shrug.

We reach my two-story building and enter through the back door. The canvas walls flex as I lead her up the dark, narrow stairs. It's sad, and poor, and it's the life I've chosen.

"I don't understand," she says, with an excited flutter in her voice. Of course she doesn't understand. She's been hurt and she's lost a lot, but it's nothing compared to what I lost in the war.

I ease off my jacket as we enter my bedroom, a square space in the air held together with rope and sailcloth. There's my bed, freshly made, a television which I never use and a glass wall looking out over the park. The red glow of an alarm clock casts a lurid glow over the neat, hollow rest of it.

"It's so empty," she says. I feel through her touch that she is crying. The engram has played havoc with her emotions.

"It's not empty now," I say. "You're here."

Her gho comes off easily, and now she's weeping against my chest. She pulls at the buckle of my belt and starts to kiss my face frantically. Her lips crush against mine and she pulls us to the bed, tugging at me so hard it hurts, squirming off her stockings, pressing her hot flesh against mine.

3. SHARK ARENA

After Mei-An leaves I lie awake for a time, watching the glow of the alarm clock flick between digits. Through the window I can just make out the half-circle encampment around the man in the moon's left eye.

These are water projects built in a bygone era, before global tsunamis on Earth swept the old order away; NASA and the Sino-Russian compact, leaving us with our Skulks and our tsunami walls. I've heard the solar reservoirs up there are as big as the great wall of Sino-Rusk. I imagine the last few humans on the lunar surface starting their own civilization built out of craters and moondust, and wonder if their lives hold any more weight than my own.

I get dressed.

It's warm out despite being some time after three, and the main alley through the Skulk is raucous, packed with a horde of boisterous Inuit offshoring in the Skulks. The smell of frying squid hangs on the salty air. The alley will chew them and their money up and spit whatever's left out soon enough.

At the alley top I cross the low-slung rope bridge into the deeper shadow of the wall, joining the flow of people on the jetty-way. A dozen Skulks pass by as I walk, each a city block-sized raft of flotation barrels lashed together, filled with bars and tattoo parlors and slums. My node beeps as I get near Carrolla.

I find him on Skulk 65 in a third-floor bar called the Aeternum, decorated like an under-ice subglacic ship with metal bolts and hatches cut from sunken boats. He's sitting at a bar made of five periscopes laid flat, shouting blearily at a man in a rubber diving suit. The bar is about half-full and I slide into a space at Carrolla's side.

"…it's a boudoir," he's shouting at the diver. "You know? An ocean-themed boudoir!"

I tap him on the shoulder. He turns and gives me a big, bleary grin. "Rit! Glad you made it." He squeezes my shoulder and calls to the barman for Arcloberry shots.

I look to the diver. I've dealt with him before, though his name escapes me. He's a salvage artist, diving the wrecks around the Skulks for useful materials. "What's he trying to buy?" I ask.

"Velour curtains," the diver says, the exasperation clear in his voice, "to line the walls of his 'boudoir'. I've told him there's not a shred of velour on any wreck I know!"

"Velvet then!" Carrolla adds. "Anything plush, to make it sexy."

The diver shakes his head. I laugh. I palm him some money and lean in close. "Get it from Calico. Tell him you dredged it up."

The diver chuckles and heads out.

"I heard that," Carrolla says sulkily, and hands me a full shot glass. "It's supposed to all be salvage."

I laugh. "You won't remember in the morning."

He grunts and knocks his shot back. I hold mine up to the light; Arcloberry vodka. The liquid is a pale purple and smells sandy, kind of like raspberry mixed with red chilis.

I love these new seed-blends, Arcloberry and the others, pleasant side effects of our War and the pack ice melting. I like to imagine all those seeds blown from the dustbowls of millennia ago trapped in the ice like hidden messages. When all the surface ice thawed and the huge blue bergs rose up from the depths, they were just the sugar frosting on the hydrate fuels underneath.

I swig it and slosh it around my mouth: a spicy berry with a kick, this message from a pre-Jurassic era. Is this what dinosaurs ate? I slot the taste into the space where the missing memory was, then rub at the reddening in my eyes.

Carrolla's already wandered off to find some girls. I've got some hard drinking to do, to get the thought of Don Zachary's son out of my mind along with all those old, sad memories of the War stirred up by Mei-An. Good thing there's a bar here, and fresh money burning a hole in my pocket.

Hours later, I come back to myself stumbling through the dark alleys of a Skulk I don't recognize, with no sign of Carrolla or the Aeternum. The rest of the night beyond that is a Lag; spotted with flashes of memory where I was drinking, flirting, maybe fighting, but nothing clear.

The usual.

My ribs and head hurt. My hands feel tacky with somebody else's blood. I touch the built-in spike in my node; clotted with blood. Abruptly it chimes, and I hold it close to my eyes but can hardly resolve the tiny screen. Arcloberry packs a punch. A message came in, but is it from Mei-An? I can't read it. Something about the Don…

"Ritry Goligh," a voice whispers nearby.

I spin to see.

What?

There's only darkness, bar the glow-light of the coming dawn over the wall. My jacket is gone and it's cool.

Did someone call my name? I turn and totter, then it comes again.

"Ritry Goligh."

I stagger after the sound, as the rising sun flashes through gaps in this Skulk's low skyline. There's a swell in the decking ahead and I climb it, following the phantom voice. Perhaps up here I'll find Ven and all my old friends from the war, and they'll still be alive, and I won't have to live this way anymore.

I crest the top and turn. An abandoned Skulk spreads around me, all jagged black shadow and sinking alleys. There's no people, no sound. I hear the voice again and take a step, then there's a sound like a gunshot as the rotten deck gives out and I fall through. For a second I tumble, then my feet smack off hard concrete, my knees punch me in the chin and I almost black out.

Lying on rough old wooden beams, I breathe in sour dust and taste my own blood. Tentatively I pat myself down for wounds, but right now it's mostly just the pain in my jaw. It'll hurt to talk for a week. Leaning to the side I vomit a little purple liquor, and feel a little clearer.

Rubbing my eyes, I peer into the darkness, lit only by the moon through the ragged hole above. There's a wide circle cut into the deck here, filled with seawater. In places the railing circling is broken inward, and there are windblown leaves crusted over the frothy scum on the surface. Perhaps ten rows of seats spread around the rail, tiered like a stadium.

A shark-fighting arena.

As with everything in the Skulks, shark fighting's not illegal, but it rarely happens anymore with sharks being so rare. I glance up to where the scoreboards would've been mounted, but see only the faint outlines of red and white wires trailing from the wall.

I went to a shark fight once, when I'd just got back from the north. It was vicious; the animals plainly starved and dying, their blood splashing across the crowd. Everybody was cheering and holding up their tickets but I felt empty, like I'd only swapped one pointless war for another.

I scan the darkness for a way out, but see none. Instead I see a man in the darkness. My heart skips a beat and my gut goes cold.

He's sitting in a ringside seat, wearing a ridiculous two-pointed hat and dressed in a dark gray suit, staring right at me. He's maybe forty years old, turning some kind of cane slowly in his hands, with eyes that are intensely white in the dark.

I flick out the spike on my node, watching him all the while, but he doesn't move.

What the hell?

"You won't need that, Ritry," he says, pointing his cane at the spiked node.

"Who the hell are you?"

He smiles broadly, displaying gleaming white teeth as bright as a shark's. "You can call me Mr. Ruin."

4. MR. RUIN

A long moment passes as he looks at me and I look at him. It's dark, and somewhere far off there is the lapping of the Arctic Ocean against this abandoned Skulk's shore.

I push myself to my feet, wavering for balance. I lean on the arena railing and almost fall in as it gives way. The metal bars slap into the water and sink slowly, cutting lines through the foam that reseal themselves like hot wax.

I gather my balance and any sense of pride, then point at this strange man in the darkness. He knows my name, which makes me feel cornered, and when I'm cornered I get aggressive.

"Your hat looks ridiculous," I say. "Take it off."

He smiles wider, and those bright white teeth blind me like boatlights. "It's not my hat," he says, his voice a warm baritone, then takes the hat off. "It's his." He points to something or someone at his feet, then drops the hat on it. There's a dark figure lying there, a long object obscured by the railing, like a body. "You should take a look at this gift. I think you'll like it."

"No, I won't," I say at once, automatically contrary. The node is comforting in my hand and I take a wobbly step forward. "How do you know my name?"

"I know a great deal about you, Ritry."

Another step forward. "That's not an answer."

My contrariness seems to delight him. "And Ritry Goligh's not a name. Who gave it to you, do you know? A clerk in the abortion hall, perhaps? The janitor, cleaning up dribbles of amniotic fluid dripping out of your machine womb? Perhaps he picked up a stub of crayon and wrote out a whim on your vat?"

I can hardly make out what he's saying, my head's too fuzzy for it, but what I'm catching I don't like. "What the hell are you talking about?"

"I think you know. I'm talking about the bath-tank that nurtured you, fed you, cycled sweet tones through the juice while you were just a scrub of organic matter waiting to be grown. Can you imagine yourself like that, Ritry, that poor, shitty cluster of cells, with no idea how unwanted it was, how pointless it was going to become as this lost, pathetic bastard I see before me?"

I laugh, spit vomit taste into the scum arena, and take another step forward. He just made it easy. "You don't know anything about me."

He spreads his arms. "Really? What do I not know, Ritry? Let me ask a question and we'll see. If you could have everything you ever wanted, everything and anything in the world, how would you feel?"

"Fuck you."

"Yes of course, but really think about it, Ritry. How would you feel?"

"I'd feel brilliant," I snap back, "with your head on a fucking pig-pole."

He smiles wide. "Liar." He says it calm and confident like he's reading facts off a node. It pisses me off, because normally I'm intimidating, at least people take me seriously, and he doesn't. I keep on forward around the curve of the shark arena but he doesn't budge.

"You need to get out of my face," I slur.

He laughs. "You're so like a fiddle when you're like this, Ritry, I swear. Easy to play. Would you like to know why you're a liar?"

"I'll carve it in your face."

He nods. "Remember you said that. Don't claim later that I didn't warn you. I am a liar to the core, Ritry, but then so are you, and I'll tell you why. Because you don't want anything at all. You may claim to, you may think you do, but what matters to you, Ritry? Nothing. You don't really feel a thing."

"You're going to feel this," I say, holding up the node. It feels heavy and slow, but it'll do the job.

He frowns. "You're not weeping yet, Ritry. Why aren't you weeping on the floor about how hard it all is, how you've lost everyone you ever cared for, to the Lag, to the ice, to the depths and shit and darkness? Why don't you weep for that poor baby you once were, because what else have you got, let's be honest? Come on, put on a show for me. Make your abandoning bitch of a mother proud."

In that instant I know I'm going to kill him.

"You're angry because you never had a mother," he goes on. "I understand that. You were aborted, flushed to a vat where they strung you along until you were old enough to fight in the ice. How do the tones go, Ritry, can you sing them for me, the ones you heard instead of a mother's pulse? Doe, Ray, Me, Far…"

The singing is what makes me see red, and finally I'm charging, stumbling, bringing the node down hard in empty air.

He's gone.

My foot snags and I drop to my knees on something solid. I find my feet again, looking around, thinking I hear his laughter but it could just be echoes of my own footfalls.

"Hey!" I shout.

"It's because I want to help you," his voice comes, and I turn. He's standing at the top of the arena now, beyond the outer ring of seats and framed by an open doorway where pink morning light is pouring in like a slow magma flow. "You'll see that too, in time. All the Mei-Ans of this world, the Dons, they're only puppets to bring us together." He grins. "It's all I want, and why I've followed you for so long, because I see the real you, Ritry. Not this hopeless, broken Soul, but what you're truly capable of, and it is magnificent. Even now you shine through the shit like a tiny sun. I would be proud to have you stand at my side, soldiers in a war that never ends, comrades against the world."

I start staggering up toward him.

"I'm offering absolution," he goes on, unphased by my slow charge, "if you can bear to reach out and take it. More than even that, though, I'm offering you a way out of this miserable malaise. I can clear out the guilt and give you something to want." A pause. "You've got a long way to go, but I'm here to help. Consider this day my gift to you. Sincerely."

My eyes blear up again and I smear them back like I'm grinding his face under my foot. "I'll kill you," I say.

He laughs. "You'll certainly try. I hope you will. I do so hope we'll become friends, equals even, in time. For now spend some time with my colleague. He'll show you I'm serious, and set you on the path."

He backs out of the entrance and the door closes behind him, plunging me back into blackness. I keep after him, but it's dark away from the hole in the roof and I bang my shins and stub my toes on the uneven steps, cursing as I go. My hand cracks off a seat back and the node clatters away over the floor but I continue up to the door.

I yank it open to find I am standing at the shoreline of this rotten Skulk, looking out over the gray-green waves of the Arctic Ocean. The sun is coming up salmon pink, like old blood swishing down the drain. It spears my spinning head and I blink against it, one hand raised to shade my eyes while I scan the Skulk-edge.

There's no sign of him.

At my feet there's a rung ladder leading down to a narrow, sun-bleached wooden walkway. It leads off along a thin jetty, half-sunk beneath the water. A few shack-like buildings rise up from it at veering angles, the water cutting them off in a diagonal line across the doorways and windows.

"Hey!" I shout, but no answer comes. I could try to chase him down, but I already dropped my node and I'm too drunk to run.

I wedge the door open with a shard of broken glass then start back down the tiered seating. With light flooding in I see the place for what it really is; a wreck. Even in life it was a place for only the dregs of humanity to come. There are broken bottles littering every surface, dark stains that must be blood splattered on floors and walls, cobwebs, the stink of bat guano. The railings and seats are all brittle faded plastic, cracked and shattered.

I find my node near the door. The glass face has maybe one more crack, but it chirps to life when I palm it. There's a call from Carrolla showing, and another from an unknown number which I guess to be Mei-An. I scrape blood out of the spike fold and depress it. It's only when I turn back to the arena that I see the body.

It's lying where Mr. Ruin was sitting; a man on his back dressed in a bizarre military uniform straight out of ancient history: white tight pantaloons with yellow trim, a deep blue vest over a white tunic with gold buttons, epaullets at his shoulders, a two-pointed hat resting over his face, and one hand tucked into his tunic over his chest.

For a long moment I stare. Not just because there's a body, but because of how he's dressed. I know who he's meant to be. As Soul Jackers we had all kinds of knowledge injected into us when we went up to face the ice, and this man was in one of them, something about strategy.

Napoleon.

A startling memory flashes up, in the way jacked-in engrams sometimes do, of two images side by side. One is of a gallant figure on a rearing horse, with a bright red cape swirling about his shoulders like a classic hero, his right hand held aloft and leading forward. The other is a mean-faced man in the rain, wearing a miserable green trenchcoat and riding a stocky brown pony, his right hand tucked into his coat. They're both the same man, but rendered by different artists.

NAPOLEON CROSSES THE ALPS

The title flashes into my mind. I lurch down toward him.

He is pot-bellied. My pulse thumps a sickly cadence in my ears as I edge up to his stockinged legs. His polished black shoes gleam in the morning light.

"Hey," I say, "wake up," but he doesn't say anything or move. I reach out tentatively to touch his left hand.

Yeah, he's dead.

I stand there and look down. The hat covers his face. I look at the seat where Ruin was sitting and surmise he must have had his feet on this man's chest. That image is hard to shake. I reach down, wary of what I'm going to find, and pluck the hat off his face.

Thank god there's no mutilation, though his neck is chafed red from the garotte that killed him. It's not Napoleon. It's just a man, blunt-nosed and ugly.

I know who it is.

Don Zachary's son.

Shit. I stare. I can't figure this out; what it means. Then Don Zachary's son begins to beep. I flinch, suddenly aware that this is how I will die, blasted apart by a bomb buried in a dead-man's fat belly, just like we bombed the crap out of the proto-Rusks with dry ice bombs stuffed in the icepack.

Boom.

But nothing happens, except the beeping continues. I set the hat to one side, stiff dark felt incongruous against the ratty plastic seating, and pat this faux-Napoleon's chest down. I have to unbutton his tunic to get to it, a tiny alarm clock clutched in his tucked-in right hand.

Underneath that there's a folder slid inside his tunic. I peel it from the cold and clammy skin of his liverworted chest with a nasty sucking sound then hold it up to the light.

RITRY GOLIGH

The words are embossed in gold on the red vinyl cover. I open it and ruffle through mismatched pages full of the same old typewriter font, interspersed with hand-scrawled maps, diagrams that look like family trees, a sketch of what looks like the earth in cross-section or perhaps a topography of the brain.

A shivery flop-sweat coats my skin. What is all this? I drank too much, fought too much. What did Ruin say? Already the sense of him is fading.

I look at the Don's dead son, Mei-An's oppressor, and wonder if he dressed up as Napoleon before he was killed or after? What must that have been like, if he'd known it was coming, like being forced to dig your own grave? Get into your coffin suit, Napoleon, you're going to make a point for me.

"Hey," I say, nudging his corpse with my foot. "I'll send someone for you."

I know as I say it that this is probably not true. I won't remember where he is, won't remember any of this in a few hours probably, with only a gleam of white teeth in the darkness and a folder of crazy conspiracy scrawlings left. I tuck it into my shirt just like Napoleon had it: touching his skin, touching mine, but so what? We all rise together, fall together. We're all the same really.

Stumbling up the stairs, I think about Mei-An, and what this means for her. I bring up my node and finally see the message she sent.

Thank you for what you did. You're a good man, Ritry Goligh. I'm sorry if you'll have to pay for my mistake.

I laugh and lurch out into the new day like some diseased wolf cub from the belly of its dead mother. What started out a pink dawn has already settled to a gray and rain-fat sky. This is all that we have now, after we blew the ice out of the Arctic.

I start down the ladder to the slap-slapping sound of the waves nudging the promontory. One good tsunami and we're all gone, I catch myself thinking. Hoping. Wash it all clean.

Over the unfamiliar terrain of that broken Skulk, I start for what home I have.

ME

A. ME

Me woke with a mouthful of smoke and hot grit in his eyes, hardly able to move, breathe, or see. He looked down at his tactical black sublavic suit, geared for war, though his chestplate was painted with spiraling yellow lines, like routes through a maze.

What?

Thoughts bubbled up from nothing, giving meaning to shape. This was his ship, he remembered, the Bathyscaphe, a sublavic vessel built to travel through the magma of a Molten Core, and he was the captain. Now something had gone very wrong. He tugged at his arms and legs but they were trapped in thick orange licks of fire, holding him in place and burning him into existence like a pot in a kiln.

"Shit!" someone shouted nearby, and he recognized the voice, Ray, though he didn't know how.

He shook his head to clear it, blinking the grit from his eyes. A corroded steel wall lay before him, a corridor. He was in a one-man pod wreathed around with flames that didn't hurt. A firing pod in the belly of the ship, he knew that much. This was where they roused when there was a mission, where they'd roused a thousand times before, but what was the mission this time?

He didn't know.

"Ray!" He shouted.

"Me, I'm burning here man!" the voice shouted back, and with the call of his name something flipped inside.

Me.

Of course that's who I am. Captain of the Bathyscaphe sublavic, even now jacking for the Solid Core with my seven-tone crew. With that remembrance comes the code to stop the forging.

lba," I say, and at once the licks of flame release, shunting me
of the pod to land on my knees on the corridor's steel floor. One
d along I see Ray stagger out of his forging bay too, then the
others beyond him. Seven of us in total; my crew.

"What the hell," Ray gasps, rubbing at his big-boned black face.
"What happened?" He's an Afri-Jarvanese I think, baked in the fires
of hell, black skin and black hair above black sublavic suit with more
yellow maze lines on the chest, in a black-tinged corridor already
filling with acrid black smoke. I smell burning clay and I feel the roll
underfoot and I know what it means.

The ship is burning off its heatproof brick cladding. Probably the
magma has already bored in through the outer layers, which is a big
problem. We're also listing at a crazy angle, so the screw must've
faltered. In short, unless I can get us to the inner surface of the
Molten Core in time we're all going to roast alive.

I get to my feet and look down the line of my crew straggled
down this worn metal corridor, from big black Ray to albino Doe,
Far just a boy, Asiatic So with her short black hair, and thin blonde
twins La and Ti holding on to each other at the end.

This is my crew; I know their names and rank even though I
don't remember anything else about them. I know how to keep them
alive though, so I start barking out orders, because that is what the
captain does.

"Ray, get to the forward trim and start flushing the tanks. Ti, eject
the screw and fire up the replacement. So and La, I want as much
cooling to the inner hull as you can muster, and Doe you're with me
for the conning tower."

The orders roll off my tongue smoothly, as though I've
commanded the Bathyscaphe every day of my life. But then I have,
haven't I? Wouldn't I remember, if I'd done anything else?

My crew lurch to their feet and get moving; Ray running down
the corridor, So and La climbing up and down into ladders I had
forgotten were there, while Ti and Doe run toward me. In the
moment before I turn to run myself, I spot Far standing still, poor
kid, alone and purposeless in the harsh metal corridor, looking
completely out of place. He doesn't have any yellow maze lines on
his black suit at all. I want to give him a teddy bear or something, but
there's no time. He shouldn't be here, but he's part of the crew too
so what choice is there?

"Hunker down, Far," I shout over my shoulder. "Ray will come
back for you." Then I jerk into motion.

I sprint along the metal corridor with the map of the ship unspooling in my head. To either side rusted pipes, ducts, dials and wiring scrawl their own map across the wall. They are polished shiny at the corners where a thousand hands have rubbed them smooth, and discolored at the seams where long years of effluents have seeped away. Even running I see all this so clearly, like it's at once the first and last memory of my life.

My booted feet thump the steel floor, echoed by Doe and Ti racing behind. The stink of burning clay is thicker now and the lurching sharpens as molten lava bites at the ship's outer layers. I adjust for the lurches well until one hits us like the Lag, tossing me bodily into the wall.

Crunch, thunk, I drop to the floor but Doe is there to pick me up. I catch a glimpse of her white brows and bleach-white face, like a lighthouse beam in my eyes, then I'm on my feet and we're running together.

"The screw must have stripped a thread," she shouts over the grinding of the engines. "Goligh knows how."

"We're in too deep," I shout back, "we'll have to punch through," then we reach the conning tower ladder and climb. I slip a glance down and see Ti is already gone, off to the deep belly to rig us a new screw. Bless Ti, I think, for she'll be the first to go.

Rung by rung I ascend, trying to make the calculations I need before I'll need them. If the replacement screw is off kilter it'll take Ti long minutes to restart, which will mean unstabilized buffeting from the deepest regions of the Molten Core. That in turn means what remains of the hull will suffer worse, and we'll begin to feel the heat even harder.

I speed up the last few rungs into the conning tower. It's the command center at the top of the ship, with a central periscope sight hanging down with handles and two glass eyes. On close-set walls assorted panels crammed with buttons flash and red lights blink and a siren blares out, showing the pattern of the emergency. Sharp-cornered desks and chairs hug the edges in discolored greenish metal; everything built-in and bolted to the floor, all cramped, angular, and utterly functional, just like me and my crew. The smell of ozone from buzzing circuitry fights with the burning clay stink. This is where I belong, where I'll get some answers. I've run a thousand missions from this spot and I'll surely run a thousand more.

I stride for the periscope, but there's a sudden thrust from the

Bathyscaphe's tail which yaws the whole ship on its nose, steepening our dive angle. I barely grab onto the periscope bars as my legs kick out with the new direction of gravity, throwing me forward.

"Ray's come through for us," Doe shouts as she pulls out of the ladder chute, holding tight to the rungs. The ship rights itself gradually and I tilt back to the floor. "He's evacuated the trim hold, buying us buoyancy."

"First tank of many," I shout back over the din of the siren, getting my feet under me. I imagine Ray deep below decks releasing great chambers of intensely pressurized ballast gas, which will drive us up faster and lighter than before. "Hold on to something." She goes to her Engine Order Telegraph bell, used to communicate orders to the decks below via a simple lever, and takes control.

I kill the siren with a single command then splay the periscope's handle rests, slot my face into the glass eyelets and look out into the Molten Core.

It's like looking into the belly of a sun. The grinding sound against the hull takes on shape as I gaze into the billowing magma of the mind. Every tremor corresponds to these swirling waves of red, yellow and orange as they radiate outward, driven by magnetic and gravometric forces of consciousness that are too huge to imagine.

We're going hard against the tide. I sweep the periscope side to side, seeking the cause. What I'm looking at is a severe magma storm, dense enough to shred all of our three brick layers at once if a wave catches us at peak. The cooling systems to the inner hull will be nothing but a brief sizzle of ice in a volcano if I can't steer us through. At least there's no sign of the Lag; it looks like we're traveling too fast even for it.

Reports ring in from all decks, called out by Doe. "Ti's jettisoned the broken screw. New one's yet to tooth to the engine."

I feel the change in the patterns of liquid rock ahead. The buffeting gets more violent as we slow.

"Tell her to make it bite now," I shout.

Another trim tank vented by Ray sends us yawing wider, almost wrenching the periscope out of my hands. I lean in and watch a great yellow wreath of molten rock bubble up toward us, wondering if this will be the one to take us out.

"So and La report the cooling's at maximum, beyond safeties," calls Doe, "in most places we've got a single layers of bricking left, the outer two are completely burned, and we're breached on several decks, with bulkheads barely standing. Ray's got three trim tanks left."

"It's only getting hotter," I call back, "we need more-"

The new engine screw bites, and I can't finish my sentence as the periscope punches me hard in the face. Stars erupt in darkness and Doe is tossed from her feet behind me.

"Backwash, clearing the gunk," Doe shouts, getting to her feet. "Me, we have to move now."

Blinking away the pain, I press my aching face back to the periscope and finally glimpse the dim outline of the Solid Core through the magma, like a fuzzy black island, visible in the scope's gamma sight.

Any port in a storm.

"Arc 23 degrees," I shout to Doe, "flanking speed, get us the hell through this."

I hear her ring out the order on the Engine Order Telegraph, two bells for direction and three sharp rings for full steam ahead. The thrum vibrates up through the floor as Ti deep below decks drives the new screw beyond capacity.

The sudden propulsion cavitates the magma ahead, and the thrust jerks me back from the periscope. Liquid rock bubbles and groans as we churn through it, moving too fast for the magma at the front to peel off, giving us a replacement heatproof layer for as long as the screw can take the pace.

"Arc 25, Hail 47, Veer 306," I call out to Doe, each navigation met by a ringing of bells through the Engine Order Telegraph system, swerving us like a leaping fish between the densest points of the lava storm. I rattle out a long stream of minute corrections that may just be enough to spare our last few layers of brick insulation and get us through. The tower around me rings with the chime of the EOT bell as Doe relays to Ti, a high trilling melody over the deep bass thrum of the Molten Core.

"Arc 23, lock it in," I finish then pull out of the periscope. We're almost to the surface and there are other things I have to do now to ensure this mission, whatever it is, will succeed. As I pull back another trim tank blows and jostles us slightly, lightening the load and speeding us on.

I stride to the display bank and tap the dial for internal cabin pressure. It's coolest here at the top, hottest down where Ti is, and not long to go. There are streams of sweat pouring off Doe already, along with a flow of blood down her chin, shockingly bright against her bright white skin.

"Bit my tongue on the last yaw," she says. "You should see your eyes, you look like a panda."

My head aches, but there's no time. We have to get out before we burn up.

"Call them all up," I say, "have Ray get Far. We'll breach the surface in T-minus ten and we need to be ready."

She aye-ayes and starts relaying my message throughout the ship. I rub my eyes and stalk toward the captain's hutch. What the hell is in the Solid Core to make this journey worth it?

B. HUTCH

The hutch lies at the back of the conning tower, down a narrow corridor lined with racks of bulky concrete Extra Vehicular Activity suits, some of which have tumbled from their racks. Beyond them the hutch is a small space with a bolted-down desk and chair for the captain to read mission orders. Embedded in the walls and ceiling are hundreds of small metal lockers, each with its own keyplate and number.

I stand in the middle and survey them. There must be five hundred in total.

Mission orders. I rack my mind for some hint of which locker is for this mission, but they all feel familiar. I have the sense that behind every one is a memory of something I've already done or have yet to do, but I don't know which one is for right now.

"Ray's here," Doe shouts over the grinding of the magma off our brick skin.

"The third layer is failing everywhere," Ray shouts. "It's gonna be close."

The ride gets rockier as we hit dregs of cooling rock near the surface, and I stare at the lockers. A mission to the Solid Core, where we've never been before, but for what? I look down at the yellow maze on my chest for clues. It looks like a schematic for a world, now that I think about it, with lines of magnetic and gravometric flow. There's also something underneath the suit, pressing against my chest. I peer down inside my armor and see a lump hanging around my neck on a leather cord. I fish it out and find a key, with a number inscribed on the side.

I find the corresponding locker wedged down in a corner. On my knees I slot the key it, turn, and the door opens. I slide out the long slim metal box within and set it on the table, unlatch the top clasp and open the lid.

There's a thick mission dossier inside, flapped with vinyl and pierced by a metal loop in the top left corner, with the usual red ink on every page that will fade when exposed. The gold-embossed title on the sleeve catches the light.

RITRY GOLIGH

The name means something to me, but I don't know what. It's a name we take in vain, like a curse, but why's it on the cover? I shove the dossier down into my armor then evacuate the captain's hutch.

The crew are gathered by the periscope, gearing up. Doe already has her huge shoulder-mounted bondless accelerator cannon on, while Ray is strapping tight the side-hammock for Far to ride in. They shove a knife in each boot, fasten elasteel coil spools to their belts wired to a grapnel-shot, holster Quantum Confusion pistols at their waists and each grab a tight ruckbag full of candlebomb, fuse, gamma-clamps and tracers.

La and So are holding hands, like La and Ti usually do, but now Ti is down with the screw and So has taken her place. La and Ti are twins, each as skilled and beautiful as the other. La's blonde hair is in a tight bun, while So with her dark hair looks like a shadow. Both of their suits are covered in pockets and patches containing every possible scientific tool we could need for a mission, while on their backs they carry larger equipment; for mass spectography, dissolution analysis and advanced mapping kit I wouldn't understand.

I nod at them. These are all professionals. These are my crew, tones hand-picked for the chord, now sweating, shaken and looking to me for guidance. I am the captain, after all. Ray gives me a tired wink. He doesn't even have a cigar stub between the silver loop piercings in his teeth, that's how bad it is.

The ship lurches again and La bleats out the report. "That'll be the second layer gone. We've minutes only."

"Where's Far?" I ask, looking around. "Where's Ti?"

Ray produces Far from behind him. The boy is terrified, and the welts in his neck are rising up again. "Give him some candy, Ray," I say, then turn to Doe. "Where's Ti?"

She says nothing. Of course we all knew this was coming.

The ship jolts again and steam pours up into the conning tower from below, filled with the overwhelming smell of sea salt and sweets baking in kilns. What? Doe is at my side, speaking in my ear.

"Ti will have to stay down there, driving the screw on or we'll sink before we even surface. All of us will sink."

I knew it the moment I sent her down there. Ti is going to die so the rest of us can live. I stride for the EOT bell and ring it backward and forward five times, enough to make it clear when no words will do.

Thank you.

Then Doe is strapping in my Quantum Confusion pistol, Ray bolts my Heads-Up-Display helmet over my head and I grab a ruckbag of gear.

Then the ship surfaces.

Everybody falls as the ship's nose jerks up through the surface of the Molten Core like a cork bobbing on water. The grind of molten stone fades a little, even as the screw deep below whines hard to keep the extra weight of us buoyant.

I pick myself up and quickly take stock. Smoke is everywhere, so thick I can barely see the others, but still I find my way to the conning tower ladder and start climbing up. Ten more rungs and I hit the exit hatch, rotate it a full revolution and open it inward.

Super-baked air pours in, scalding my lungs, and I slam my HUD's visor into place. "Screen your eyes," I shout down at the chord. My HUD display grays instantly, blocking the worst of the magma glare glowing through the brick.

"Pick," I shout down, and Ray hands me up the pickaxe. It's hard to wield in this tight space, but it has to be done. The inner hull of brick is mortared in place like the wall of a house, the last thing between the outside and the baking interior of this dying ship.

I drive the pick into the brick and red clay shards spit out. A chunk of mortar clatters off my visor. Sweat stings in my eyes and I swing again, taking a sizable divot out of the inner hull, and catch a taste of the extreme heat without.

Two more blows, this time with the suit's exo-muscles engaged, and the bricking tumbles down around me. I climb up through the hole, onto a blackened crag of sinewy black magma crust, cooling now atop the back of the Bathyscaphe.

Around me is the all-encircling glory of the Molten Core; a burning, curving sea of fire. In every direction the molten flows spread outward and upward, red and orange with a crust of dirty black in places, arcing around to rejoin far overhead in a perfect globe. We are but a dark outcropping on this churning, encircling ocean, a burned ship's nose on the inner surface of a vast sphere walled with lava.

I don't think I've ever seen this before.

"Holy shit," Ray says. "It's like climbing up into hell."

He's right. It is no place for people, not even marines. I look directly up and see a great moon of black rusted metal hanging at the center, pitted as though with old meteor strikes. We have breached the surface of the Molten Core to reach it.

The Solid Core.

I've heard legends, I know stories, but there's no content to any of them. I've felt it all my life, pulsing away at the edge of the thousand missions I've run, but I've never seen it before. It is immense. It hangs at the very heart, encircled by a moat of air and suspended by nothing, just existing.

"Ho-ly shit," Ray repeats. "That is a humdinger."

So and La climb up beside us, followed by Doe. Of course there is no Ti. Each of their faces shows the awe they're feeling to be here, except Doe, who stares only at me expectantly.

I nod. "Work the grapnels," I tell her. "Get us off this thing."

The Bathyscaphe grumbles underfoot, and I know the screw is dying under the ship's immense weight. There is no way Ti can make it out now. But who is Ti anyway? I have no real memories of her, and perhaps this is why. I saw her once down the corridor, and then she died so that the rest of us could live. She is an idea that has served its purpose, and her death is as certain and complete as any death in history.

I pat the mission document tucked against my chest, hold onto Far tight and watch as Doe fires her grapnel line to the Solid Core. It whips upward, uncoiling rapidly from the spool at her waist. The grapnel crosses the gulf, bites into the Core and locks, then Doe begins latching us all onto the taut line even as the ship sinks underfoot. Its metal walls buckle with a deep scream beneath the heat, like a crumpling tin can, and its final brick hull melts away. It starts to sink downward and we sink with it, inching back to the molten flows which birthed us.

Goodbye Ti, I think, as Doe starts the grapnel incoil and my feet lift off the ship's crusted black back. It should be the captain who goes down with the ship, I think, not the engineer. Goodbye Ti, goodbye Bathyscaphe.

We rise into the air in a clump and I watch my sublavic sink. Perhaps I am crying, as it folds slowly into the burning waves. Magma flows into the hole I hammered through its brick and mortar back, and I can only hope the end for Ti will be quick. Probably she will choke on exhaust though, as the magma burns up all the air. Then she will bake, then she will crumple as the walls bend inward, and then she will burn.

Below me the ship is swallowed and gone.

I look up, my body nudging against Ray and So as we rise. The ragged black bulk of the Solid Core grows massive overhead.

This is why we have come.

C. SOLID CORE

The Solid Core changes as we draw in; no longer a moon-like sphere, it becomes a black ceiling with a slightly convex horizon, broken by uneven struts, chaotic metal gables and strange bracing stanchions, like it was welded by a child. We web ourselves to it through large rivet-holes in its ancient, rusted girders. Up close the surface is pitted and corroded, etched with dozens of graffiti messages from those who've come before.

CARROLLA WAS HERE

FERRILY TIGRATES HECLAN

RG + VEN 4EVA

Who were these people? I wonder, as I run my gloved fingers over the marks they've left behind. Were they like Ti, marines who could never make it any further, who died to bring us this far?

I should stop thinking about her; I don't even remember anything about her more than a flash of dark hair. I have responsibilities to the living.

I give orders to Doe, La and So for a patrol to recon the Solid Core, and they start at once; shooting their grapnels to the next beam of girders, hooking in on elasteel line and traversing the rough black ceiling through low arcing swings.

Now Far is tucked in beside me, sitting on the lip of a Solid Core girder, and Ray is singing him a simple song. Ray is good at this kind of thing.

Looking down there's the sea of Molten Core below, yellow striped with red like muscle fibers. Orange bubbles of liquid rock burst lazily on the surface. I touch my chest above the mission document tucked into my combat suit and wonder about its meaning.

Ritry Goligh.

It's a name, but who? Not one of my marines or anyone I know, more like a kind of distant concept like god or the devil. I intend to read the pack as soon as both my lieutenants are present, to catch everything we can before the ink disappears.

"Do you know someone called Ritry Goligh?" I ask Ray.

He stops singing to Far and looks to me with a raised eyebrow. "No. He sounds familiar though. Who is he?"

"I don't know. Title of the mission pack."

He nods. "You found it then."

"Yeah."

He gives me a blank look. "I shouldn't say this, since I'm your second lieutenant, but I don't even know what this mission's for, Me." A long pause. "Do you?"

I don't, not any more than him, but I'm the captain and can't show that indecision. "Enter the Solid Core."

"OK, but beyond that? I don't remember anything before waking up in the sublavic, though I know who you are, and the others. Even this kid," he nudges Far. "I know we're a team, we've worked together before, but I don't know why."

"We're a chord," I say. "It hurt me to lose Ti too."

Ray looks away. "A chord, yeah. I didn't even speak to her."

I don't know how I know Ray. I couldn't name his birthday or what city he's from, but I do know that this is a way he grieves, as if we've already seen a thousand deaths together.

"Do you think it's an effect of the forging," he asks, "this loss of memory?"

I think back to those first moments in the sublavic, trapped in the forging fire and not knowing who or what I was. "I can't really remember ever being forged before. I've got nothing to compare it to."

Silence holds between us for a while, broken only by the distant flare and fizz of magma below. I feel uneasy; like there's something I'm supposed to be doing, but I don't know what it is.

I pull out the mission pack. The hot wind flutters its pages, and I hook an elasteel line from my belt through the binding hole in the corner. It clanks satisfyingly. I look over the red cover with its mysterious RITRY GOLIGH in gold, feeling the weight of it in my hands.

"You should wait to share it with Doe," Ray says.

"I will," I answer, and I turn the blood-mic comms system on. I barely need to vocalize the sound, as the blood in my body captures the vibrations in my throat and transmits them through the reader over my heart. "Doe, I'm going to read out loud the first page of our mission brief."

"Agreed," she answers.

I lay my suited fingers at the hermetically sealed edge of the pack, peel back the first page like skin sucking off a fresh orange, and open my mouth to read.

DO NOT READ THIS ALOUD

ONE OF YOUR CHORD WILL KILL YOU ALL

I say nothing, instead closing my mouth as the words swiftly fade from red to pink, from pink to nothing.

"Well?" says Doe through the comm.

Ray is looking at me with a mixture of amusement and surprise, like this is a much better game than singing to Far.

"We'll wait, on second thoughts," I say sheepishly. "Keep up the recon. Out."

Ray chuckles. "That's embarrassing."

"It's unnerving," I say. "How did the writer know I would read it out loud?" I turn over the pack and look at the back as if there might be answers there.

"Maybe they didn't. Maybe it's standard. How many of these have you opened before?"

I strain to remember, because I know I've opened some, but where and when? Was I infiltrating then as well? Was it in the depths of the Molten Core, or some sunken one?

I tuck the pack back into my suit.

"So who do you think is the traitor?" Ray asks. "Who's going to kill us all?"

"It could be you," I say.

"Or it could be you."

There's not much more to say after that. Ray goes back to his lullabyes and I look down into the molten blaze below, trying to think back on everything I know about the others, but there's nothing. Names, a few traits, a sense about them perhaps, but that's all. We could be complete strangers for all I know, not even tones in the same chord at all.

D. CHARGER

Ten minutes in, and there's a growing sense of unease writhing like a worm in the pit of my stomach. Nothing feels right in this place, not the chord or the mission. I need to look after my people, but who are they? Who amongst them would kill us all?

The mission pack grows clammy against my chest, too hot and too cold at once. We have to read it. We have to move. We have to get this mission done.

I switch on blood-mic. "Report," I order.

"Nothing yet," Doe comes back, her voice a fuzzy crackle. "I'm past the far pole."

"So?"

"Nothing either, just girders."

"La?"

A moment passes before La replies. "Perhaps. I'm running a depth gauge now. It's not a door, but there's writing carved into the metal in the outline of a gateway. It's written in a different language; I think Gaullic."

A chill runs up my spine. By my side Far shudders and Ray tamps him down with soft words.

"What does it say?"

"'Arrete! C'est ici l'Empire du Mort.' It keeps repeating. Do you know what that means?"

I don't. Doe speaks into the silence. "It means 'Stop, this is the Empire of the Dead.'"

The line goes quiet for a moment. Why not, I wonder? No one knows what the Solid Core is.

"What do the depth gauges say?"

"They say…" A pause while she checks. "Nothing. The material's impenetrable to all radiation."

Another chill. That's not supposed to happen. It's what the depth gauges are meant to bypass. We'll have to do it the old-fashioned way. "Try hitting it," I say. "Sound it for hollowness."

She does, and her suit's external mics capture the sound of it; a hollow bonging like some old clock tolling time.

I look at Ray, and he gives a nod. He feels it too, that we can't stay here any longer; like the longer we stay the less real we become.

"It's our way in," I say, "we'll blast it. Doe and So, end the recon and head to La."

They Roger it.

Ray clicks blood-mic to a private channel. "Not *the* way in, if it's sealed off," he says. "Somebody doesn't want us coming in."

"Who ever wants to see us, Ray?"

He grunts. It's not really a joke. I don't remember seeing anyone other than the chord, ever.

"None of this feels right," Ray says, and pulls his grapnel. I can't argue with him.

"You first," I say.

He nods, his sharp green eyes already looking into the distance, and fires. A percussive slap smacks the air as his grapnel shoots off to loop around another girder far along the Solid Core's curved horizon.

"See you at the Deathgate, Me," he says, locks the grapnel line in to his suit and shuffles off the girder.

Together he and Far fall. The rope catches them and they arc down like a pendulum. The boy's long wail calls out like a siren fading, growing deeper until they are just a black dot against searing lava.

I look back once more to the lava where we lost Ti, and can't help but feel that I'm aleady less, like I'm leaving a part of myself behind. Yet the rest of the chord lies ahead, and I'm responsible first to them.

I fire my grapnel, the head snags on a girder and I fall.

The Solid Core recedes, the lava of the Molten Core screams up at me then the line catches and pulls me into my own pendulum swing. Hot air rushes over my HUD, exhilaration drives out the cramp of waiting and then the tracer in my suit begins the in-reel. In seconds I'm sitting on the latch-point, refastening my cables to fire. Ray is there grinning widely through his visor.

"You never said it was this much fun, Doe," he says on blood-mic.

Doe comes back as flat as ever. "Say it's fun after fifty more swings."

Ray's grin only widens. "The only way to travel," he says through blood-mic, then drops again.

It is less than fifty swings to the Gaullic markings. We pull up to find Doe, So and La hanging from a brace of wires strung between girders.

"Welcome to the Deathgate," says La.

I lean in to study the 'gate'; the carving truly is remarkable. The Gaullic words are arrayed around a neat rectangle, like a picture frame. Each letter is as big as my shin, and scored so deeply into the black that they shimmer silver.

I reach into one of the depressions. "What alloy is this?" I ask, flicking up my HUD and looking at So. The magma-heated air burns hot on my skin.

"Something poly," she says, brushing black hair out of eyes, "and impossible. La?"

I turn to La. She looks mildly distraught. We're all feeling it, I think. "The readings don't make sense, Me. These atoms seems to be bound not with the strong force, but with gravity itself."

I frown. My molecular chemistry is weak, but not that weak. All elements are bound by the so-called strong force, as compared to the weak force of radioactive decay, the magnetic force, and gravometric bonds. "How can it be anything but the strong force?"

La reaches between the tangle of our bodies, hanging ungainly there like bats in hammocks, to pass me a readout. I look at it and see numbers. "This just says its gravometric, which is macro-scale; we're talking planets, correct?"

She nods. "Correct. What we're looking at are gravometric bonds working at an elemental level."

"It's not possible, we know," Doe says, "it shouldn't exist, but here it is."

"What does it mean?" I ask.

Doe shrugs, enough of a motion to start us all bobbing on the cables. "What it comes down to, is there might be a black hole on the other side of this metal."

I almost laugh. "A black hole?"

"Could be," Doe repeats.

The urge to laugh dwindles. "Can we blow it?"

"We can, but it'll take most of our candlebomb and almost all our fuse. We can't be anywhere near this spot when the blast goes up.

The whole Core could lose integrity. If it is a black hole we'll just get spaghettified in an instant. But if it's something else…" she trails off.

I look around at the chord. Ray has flicked up his HUD and is running his swarthy fingers inside the carved metal letters.

"Who would write something like this?" he says quietly.

I look back to Doe. We're marines after all, and this is our mission. "Set it up."

Doe sets to work, while the rest of us swing away to a safe distance. Soon Doe is with us, pressed next to Ray with strands of her white hair pasted to her damp cheeks. Ray leans over to peel one errant hair away, and she eyes him curiously, as though she can't quite comprehend what he's doing.

"Excuse me," he says, "you had a bit stuck."

Doe raises an eyebrow then holds out the fuse. I nod. "T-minus ten," she says, and sparks it with the gasjet barrel of her rifle. Far wriggles by my side and Ray pats his head. I see So and La are holding hands again. Ray takes Doe's free hand in his own and she pulls it casually away. The spark races up the fuse like a shooting star and we all tighten our grip on the metal.

BOOM

The spark strikes the candlewax and the explosion bursts like a lava bloom. Black shrapnel blows out and down in a broad trajectory, a fireball inflates then with a staccato snap sucks back into itself.

A tsunami of sound crashes over us though my HUD quickly renders it silent, then the pressure wave hits and we all sway. Throughout I keep watch on the Core, barely breathing as the initial light and smoke dissipate, so that when a shape falls out from inside I see it clearly.

A man on a white horse, dressed in a dark blue tunic with brightly burnished buttons that caught the magma like lens flare. He holds a shining silver rapier blade in his hand and there is dark blood on his bright white pantaloons, embroidered with yellow thread. Spurs glint on his long black boots as he spins down to the magma.

"Charger!" he shouts, the sound reaching me seconds before the lava claims him.

I let my jaw go slack and turn to Doe.

"Gaullic," she says, her voice a cracked whisper. "It means charge, as in attack."

I look back to the smoking hole in the Solid Core and wonder what madness lies within.

RITRY GOLIGH

5. POWER

I wake in the afternoon with a pale gray light rinsing through the window of my apartment. The sky is brain-matter gray; rain clouds rolling over the Arctic Ocean. The smell of Mei-An is on the sheets still and one of her dark hairs shimmers on the pillow, but she is of course long gone.

I hurt.

Bruises on my face and cracked ribs tell a story of violence, and with it come intermittent memories of last night; Carrolla, and a fight, and wandering through some ruined Skulk where a dead body wearing a familiar face waits, and the long trek home.

My breath stiffens involuntarily.

A hot shower helps with my throbbing head. My node rings and I ignore it, probably Carrolla calling me to the jack-site. In my miserly kitchenette I locate the seaweed bread and force down two slices, then I look at the folder on the table before me.

From Napoleon's tunic. I remember that much. Don Zachary's son. It's a red vinyl folder titled RITRY GOLIGH in embossed gold. It holds maybe a hundred yellowed pages of different sizes scrawled over with inky notes.

'This is my gift to you,' Mr. Ruin said. I remember his eyes, his teeth and the almost magical way he fled from my spike.

He killed Don Zachary's son. He sent Mei-An to me. I don't understand any of it.

I pick up the folder and open it to the first paper, handwritten, and begin to read.

MCAVERY'S SHARK-FIGHTING ARENA

SKULK 53, QUAYSIDE

I recognize it; it's where I ended up last night. Beneath the title and location is a map and a summary:

Abandoned 2355, when the last tsunami warning came.

I blink, remembering that warning. I was only three months out of the Arctic then, still wandering the streets every night looking for something I couldn't find, burning through my War bounties in women and liquor.

A second birth for you, wasn't it, Ritry?

This line, scrawled in red ink beside the title, must be from Mr. Ruin. But how would he know that?

Back then half the people fled the Skulks in fear, paying everything they had to broach the tsunami wall into Calico. I never considered it; I was in the place I belonged. On the eve of the wave I sat at the edge of Skulk 1 with a crowd of other lost Souls, and together we waited for the wave to come wash us away.

"Arctic?" a man to my right had asked. I could see he was a marine from the deadness in his eyes.

I nodded. He pointed at himself. "Desert. Tar sands."

That explained everything. He'd fought the new coalition nations in the sand, and I'd fought them in the ice. Perhaps we were on the same side, or opposite sides, but what did that matter to either of us then?

"You're a Soul Jacker," he said, again reading it in me, as I read in him he was an arene engineer. Once he'd roved the Hollow Desert or the Darain sands in his massive suprarene tank, boring down to scavenge cities lost beneath the dunes.

"I was."

He pointed a thumb to the left. "The Jacker on Skulk 47 ran. His place'll be free, if you can use it."

And that was all. There were criminals and killers all around us, god knew I was one, but we sat together and waited for the wave, gambling our lives on the weather. It was a high point and a turning point, the air thick with lost dreams and resignation. When the wave never came, it only seemed natural to move to the abandoned jack-site and start implanting memories. I've been there ever since.

And somehow Mr. Ruin knew.

I read on. Next come three paragraphs describing the shark arena; a potted history like something I could pull up on my node for any spot in Calico, though of course there are no records for places like this, out in the Skulks.

It was owned by a man named McAvery, who started it with his bounty from the War as part of a dream to breed sharks to hunt porpoise. His dream failed. Instead he converted the podding bays into an arena and found a modest level of success starving his sharks into fighting.

Somewhere in there he lost his way, and started to beat his wife and his daughters until they fled him. He became a rageful drunk, so deeply sickened by the deterioration of his dream that he grew cruel. He had loved the sharks, but now he tortured them every night for crowds he despised. Soon he made the fights more ferocious, longer and drawn-out, as though he was plumbing for the lowest ebb he could reach. The crowds correspondingly grew larger. What else was there to do?

On the night of the wave he burned himself alive, taking half the Skulk down with him in an inferno which ironically left his most hated creation, the arena, completely untouched. At the bottom of the page there is another note in red pen.

There is power here, Ritry, if you dare to take it.

I set the papers down.

What? I don't know what he's talking about, power. What power? At the same time though, there's a hint of something there. A feeling, maybe, hidden in the black spots of the fog of the night and lost within my drunken mind. A certain feeling from Mr. Ruin, maybe, in the moments when he seemed to disappear then reappear somewhere else.

What happened? I've never seen anything like it. The uncertainty scares me and I begin to doubt my own memory, which makes the decision easy. I need to know for sure.

I dress, slip the red folder into my jacket, and look over my sad apartment. This will be a ruin too someday, like McAvery's dream, crushed beneath the next great wave and driven to the bottom of the ocean. Divers will come to pillage my room for velour. Will Mr. Ruin scrawl an entry on a piece of paper about me and my forgotten life?

Is there power here too?

I step out the door.

6. HERO

Mid-morning, and the crulls are flocking through the blue tarp park as I stride by. The homeless marine is out and so is a mad old woman tossing seaweed crumbs. I watch them at their efforts as I circle the sagging lake of algae-scummed rainwater.

The Skulk's main alley is quiet at this time. One of my favorite ladies waves at me from her window, two stories up in a wooden brothel, and I wave back. The jack-site is open. Carrolla is standing at reception poring over the reservation book, not looking hungover at all. He looks up when I come in and flashes me a grin.

"Conquering hero," he says, "I heard about your exploits."

I give a faint smile. I have no idea what he's talking about, but that's nothing new after a heavy night. "I saw yours firsthand," I counter, tapping into a lucid bubble of memory. "Did you take both of those girls home?"

"I took them to the bar." He pauses. "And there were three."

I can't help but laugh. In all likelihood he spent hours explaining every detail of his 'bar' to them, which is currently a lean-to scaffold made of sea-bamboo, largely floorless and without a hint of alcohol in sight. I doubt any of the girls stayed long enough for romance to happen, though in the past some girls have found his passion for the project intoxicating. Perhaps they're imagining all the cash he'll one day make while slinging whiskey to freightermen.

"I heard you fought off a gang off Armoricans," he says. "You OK?"

I try for a smile. Is that who I fought? "Maybe. Aches and pains. I met a weird guy." I don't know how else to explain Mr. Ruin. "I don't remember much more, so I'm going to self-jack."

Carrolla narrows his eyes. It's not normal, but I've done it once or twice before; times I thought I'd seen Ven or one of my old marines in the middle of a heavy bender. Of course I couldn't have, because they're all dead. But still.

He just shrugs. "You're the boss."

Five minutes later I'm lying down on the EMR input tray in the jack-room. Self-jacking is a lot easier than syncing up with another mind, but there are still risks. The Lag exists in my head just as it does anywhere else; go deep enough or stay long enough and it'll consume me just as surely as it consumes any other intruder.

"Firing it up," Carrolla says, and the EMR starts to thump. I close my eyes as the electromagnetic soup builds, the tray shunts me in and I start the jack.

The mind is like a planet, I've come to understand. Cut it in cross-section and you'll see concentric rings. The tough outer layers are like the planet's crust, followed by thousands of miles of dirt, rock and metal, which correspond to knowledge banks, muscular control, nerve centers and all the necessary systems that make a person work.

Beyond that lies the Molten Core, the home of conscious thought, embodied for me as a deep ring of burning magma. This is where the Lag begins its guardianship, and the site where any engram or new memory must first be absorbed before entering long-term storage. It's where I've spent all of my professional life as a Soul Jacker, navigating those dangerous flows.

Nestled within the center of the Molten Core lies the Solid Core, a hard, mysterious dot in the middle of the mind. Some researchers say it's the seat of the soul, but for most it's just a myth. To even get near it requires intimate knowledge of every inch of the Molten Core. The Lag is stronger there, and can eat a Soul Jacker in a single gulp.

I know my own mind better than any. I've jacked deeper and longer than anybody else alive, close enough to glimpse the Solid Core through the inner surface of the magma, but I've never gone inside. Nobody ever has, though many have Lagged themselves trying. It's the brain's final mystery, and within it may lie the key to all divinity, or the seed of sentience, or perhaps nothing at all, merely a fixed point about which all else revolves.

I don't need to go that deep to recover last night. I jack in and find the memory captured as a pattern of electrical pulses stored across my visual and auditory centers. It's grimy, and I isolate it for cleaning with a blast from the sublavic ship's sonic cannons, then I set my team of seven working to pick out its contours, like archaeologists salvaging an ancient piece of pottery from the earth.

In the memory, I see and hear Mr. Ruin with crystal clarity. Sitting in the darkness of McAvery's arena, resting his feet on Don Zachary's dead son dressed in Napoleon's clothes, I hear again what he has to say: insults, challenges, strange ideas. He suggests he was responsible for Mei-An and boasts of knowing me in ways that aren't possible; he hopes I'll try to kill him and that somehow we'll still be friends; then he does something I've never seen before, outside of an EMR.

He Lags me.

Within the magma of my own Molten Core I watch the memory play through again. In the moment I remember it felt like disappearing; a blip where he was one moment here, the next moment there, but now I see it is not that.

It was an actual Lag of my memory. I can feel it still, as I inhabit again my own skin for those seconds in the lead up, charging with my spiked node out. The electromagnetic soup rises up around him in a split second, as if generated by an invisible Electro-Magnetic Resonance machine, then the memory just snips. Content and frame both are gone, leaving an uneven join where the memory halves have been slotted together again.

I stare at the memory of his face, standing at the top of the stairs and haloed by the pink dawn beyond. It isn't possible. Souls can't be Jacked outside of an EMR. But then what...

I run it again. I lean in and really listen to the changes as he works them. Something in the air around him is responding. In moments only the electromagnetic medium appears, but it doesn't come from him. I can be certain of that, because I can feel him coaxing it out of thin air.

It is impossible.

I replay it and delve closer, but there is nothing to see except the trimmed edges. Seconds lost, perhaps. Minutes, maybe, but no way to know. I watch in wonder at this phenomenal magic trick. I watch five times more, then lock the cleaned memory back in place and give the signal for the sublavic to surface.

I need to think, and the Lag is already circling tight. The trim tanks release their pressurized ballast gas and the ship rises up through the molten lava of consciousness, until at the edge we encounter a block. This is not uncommon, as random shiftings of the mind can shift the boundaries around, cutting off an entry path. I reverse course and try for another exit, one through the nerves for my left hand, but find a block there too.

Strange. I try another, out through a memory of Mei-An, but that is blocked too. Another and another still are blocked, and I begin to worry. I've been trapped like this before and it almost killed me. The Lag is close on my trail.

"Carrolla," I shout inside my sublavic, with all the crew calling at once. "Carrolla!"

Once when jacking the Soul of an enemy marine in the Arctic, searching for secrets on resources and their deployment of force, I got trapped in his mind when our ship was attacked and my EMR operator was killed. I survived for half a day inside the man's dying mind before someone shut the EMR down.

The man was dead, because I gave up everything he had to the Lag. I gave up half of myself too, everything I ever knew, just to stay alive. I was a zombie for months afterward, re-learning how to do the simplest of motor actions; elementary skills I'd sacrificed to save the core frame of my mind, while adjusting to the gaping wounds in my memory.

The Lag remembers this, too. It has a taste for me already, and already I feel it rooting behind my sublavic, teeth snapping at the fins. I spin on, racing around the Molten Core like a ricocheting bullet, looking for the way out, while members of the crew begin preparing a walk through Carrolla's half-built bar as the first sacrificial offering.

'Carrolla!' I shout through the link. 'Carrolla!'

Finally the outer surface yields and I burst through. I jerk onto my elbows with a gasp inside the EMR machine as its thumping sound cycles down. I see a restraining hand on my chest, but it's not Carrolla's. I blink, then the hand drags me down the input tray and out of the machine, to look up into the blunt-nosed face of Don Zachary himself.

7. FINGERS

He's an ugly old man with cataract-rheumy eyes and a craggy red alcoholic's nose. As ever, he wears an outfit that looks like pajamas, bright red and purple like he's just gotten out of bed. He's as vicious as anyone I ever met in the Arctic, and last night I found his dead son.

"Where is he?" he asks.

I blink and push against the stubby hand holding me down. It relents, letting me sit up, but there is nowhere to go. There are three of them in the room, big guys I've seen escorting the Don around before. At the operator's panel is Carrolla, his face turned white with a bloody clump of tissues held to his hand.

Oh no. He lifts the tissue away to reveal his index finger is missing. It has been replaced by a long rusty nail, driven into the wound.

Holy shit. It's horrific and comical at the same time, like he's turned part mechanical scarecrow. I feel my gorge rise. The poor bastard is so pale.

"Sorry, Rit," he says weakly. I don't know how he's even conscious. "They wouldn't let me bring you up."

I turn back to the Don. All the stories are true; I never doubted that. Now I have to play this right if either of us is going to survive. Whimpering and begging won't mean a thing to him. A finger swapped for a nail and some Lag-time are really just his way of saying hello.

"Don Zachary," I say, forcing a smile. "What a pleasure. Can I offer you a cup of tea?"

He doesn't smile. In the past, on the few occasions he's come by to collect his tithe in person, he's seemed amused by my cheeky irreverence, but plainly not now. I dump it.

"Where is he?" the Don repeats, holding up what can only be Carrolla's finger. He wags it at me. "Tell me what you know or your boy'll not get this back. I might even take a few more."

I try to fake it. I'm a good liar. "Where's who? I don't know who you're talking about."

The Don looks at me a long moment, then sets the bloody finger down by my side. "My son. He's been here for collections before, as ugly as me but fat too. You know him."

The memories are all there now, freshly cleaned. Don Zachary's son is as clear as ever in my mind, dressed in death as Napoleon Bonaparte.

"I haven't seen him. I don't know."

The Don frowns, though there's a hint of a smile about it, as though this is something he enjoys. "I know you jacked one of his girlfriends last night. Mei-An? You like to play the white knight, I see that, to rescue the maiden fair? You screwed her, OK, I could even forgive that, but now both her and my boy are gone and that requires an answer. Where is he?"

Another piece clicks into place, about Mei-An and her DZ tattoo, explaining why a Calico Reach girl would come here of all places for a Soul-jack. There were parts of herself she kept hidden, and I didn't pry. This was the reason.

My thoughts swirl like blood down the drain. Mr. Ruin's set me up. Mei-An, the son, the Don. I'm in his game now.

I look up at the Don, unable to get the disbelief out of my eyes. The Don nods sagely, seeing only what he wants. "Take another finger," he says.

After the screaming, Carrolla stares dumbfounded at the two nails in his hand. They shift faintly as he works his remaining fingers. That's when he vomits, but they don't let him leave. The smell makes me sick, too, with the hangover still sweating off and only stale liquor and seaweed bread in my gut.

"Once more with feeling," says the Don calmly, belying the calm, procedural violence we've all just witnessed. "You've got to understand I'll do anything to get my son back. He's a fat shit who sticks his dick where it isn't welcome, I'll admit that, but he's my son. There's such a thing as respect. What did you do?"

"I didn't do anything. I swear it."

Don Zachary considers. "Would it help if we took your fingers instead of his? Something else perhaps?" He waggles his pinkie.

"God, no," I whisper, trying to calculate how much to act and how much to show. "I didn't do anything. The girl came for a Soul jack, you're right, and sex is part of the contract, but that's it. I didn't know she was your son's. I went out drinking afterward."

He frowns. "You're a Soul Jacker and you didn't know? And seems you got yourself beaten up pretty bad?"

I look down at the bruises on my arms. I know my face must be puffy and dark around the eyes. This is condemnation. "It was freighters, asshole Armoricans in some end-Skulk bar."

Zachary frowns. "Not a man fighting for his life?"

"Why would I want to kill your son?"

The Don shrugs. "You fell in love with his little bitch, maybe? What's her name?" He turns to one of his hulking men, who whispers in his ear. "Mei-An, that's it. I heard about her climbing over the tsunami wall with a head full of new knowledge. You were helping her escape, yes, a lovers' pact, but you couldn't leave without paying my son back, a little off-book justice? Will we ever find his body? Did you burn him or sink him?"

"I wouldn't be such an idiot. I didn't even touch him."

The Don surveys me with a new interest. "Really? Now, you had me until that. But that was a very specific lie, wasn't it? Now I'm interested."

One of his men hands him a bat, and without any warning he slams it into my stomach. I barely have time to tense before it lands and it drives all the air out of my lungs. I gag on my own spit, cough and try to curl up over the pain but they won't let me. It hurts so bad I can't think.

"I'm not playing around here, son," says the Don, toying with the bat. "Tell me everything you know, or you and your boyfriend are going to be stroking each others' dicks with nails for the rest of your short, miserable lives. Now."

I concede this has gotten beyond my ability to control. I tell him everything that I know; about Mei-An, his son dressed as Napoleon, the shark-fighting arena and Mr. Ruin.

8. SKULK 53

They let Carrolla pick up his fingers, drop them in an icebox and flit off for the nearest hospital. There are several on the neighboring Skulks. He'll have no problem getting credit, because they'll know I'm good for it. Whether the Don's men will actually let him get any further than the front door and out of my sight though, I do not know.

Me they hold on to. Out of the jack-site, we turn left down the sad alley to the grimy plastic-mat jetty. Shored off the edge is a gleaming white speedboat.

"I believe you," the Don says, standing beside the speedboat. He looks strange in his pajamas, here on the battered Skulk's fringe. "I could get some other Calico jacker in here to jack you for confirmation, but then you know that don't you? If we don't find what you've promised, I expect I will. Now, after you."

His thugs in dark suits manhandle me onto the boat. Perhaps I could drop one of them, if I had my spiked node. Maybe I could handle all three if I was in peak condition, but I'm pretty far from that and they know it. I'm hungover and in shock, can hardly get my wind back after that single blow to the stomach, and they have guns.

"Mr. Ruin," says Don Zachary, reclining in a leather-padded chair facing the speedboat's nose, while I hunch unceremoniously on a storage box facing the engine. "It's too strange to make up."

He leafs through Mr. Ruin's folder as his bodyguards unmoor the boat, holding up a hand to stop them from starting the engine. An interesting part, I guess. We all wait, cramped and uncomfortable in the boat, until he looks up at me with a strange light in his eyes.

"I think we're doing you a favor here, son. Looks like this guy has a major hard-on for you. You'd have been wearing your kidneys like bloody pompoms in a couple of days, if not for us."

I nod. I'm not about to argue with anything he says, now.

"And now he's gonna die, hard. All things come, you know."

He gives the signal and the speedboat engine roars to life, black scum fountaining up from the propeller as we lurch forward. I barely just catch my balance on the speedboat's side.

The Don is impassive, studying the folder as the boat races into a choppy glide over the water.

"I am sorry about your son," I say.

He waves a hand. "Don't be. I have others."

Infamously, he does. It's one reason I didn't recognize the man posed as Napoleon earlier: the Don is rumored to have over one hundred children. To my knowledge they are all exactly as ugly as their father.

"I don't know why this Ruin got you tangled up in this," I go on, "or why I'm involved either."

"He's mad," says the Don disinterestedly.

The boat whips over the waves with a thumping regularity. The spray of Skulks grows clearer as we get some distance, like dark bacterial growth clinging to the Calico tsunami wall. At last count I think there were ninety Skulk barges in proto-Calico, but that number is constantly in flux. There's always one foundering, its flotation barrels failing, with one going up in flames and another being added. There are always boats getting rigged into the mix as well, in the gaps between the Skulks: yachts, coracles, catamarans, schooners, deck-frigates, in one place I believe there's an old Ananzi-Rusk subglacic. Some charge tolls as new bridges while others offering some variation of bars, barrios and brothels.

It makes the Skulks a feverish, ever-shifting place: a proto-city for proto-people all living in the shadow of the next global tsunami.

The Don continues leafing through the folder. "Did you know that the godship fleet wrecked on hidden reefs somewhere near here?" He doesn't look up. "I thought they were totally destroyed."

"I didn't know," I say, "I hadn't read that far."

"Might be good plunder there. I'll send a crew."

I look out to sea. In that direction there is only the gray of waves, spiked in places by a few hydrate mines like spinning tops on the horizon. Here and there I catch the green of a kelp farm. Go the distance a few hundred miles after that and you'll be at the Arctic Pole, where once there was ice.

I watch the Don, intent on his reading. There is no hint in his wrinkled old eyes of whether I'm to die today or not. I consider throwing myself off the boat, but it would do no good. They'd only swing around and pick me up again, maybe chop off a few of my fingers and drive in nails.

Or something worse.

Soon the charred exterior dock of Skulk 53 rushes by on our left. In some places the framework is gone entirely, in others the bones of it still remain, splintered with blackened metal girders. The speedboat pulls up to the flagging dock. I remember it, half-sunken and lined with a few tilting bars. From this angle the shark arena looks like a bloated mushroom, its once brown exterior faded with the rain to a sleety gray. It's a wonder it never burned along with the rest of this doomed Skulk.

The engine kicks out and a silence falls over the dead Skulk and us. Perhaps respectful of this, the Don's thugs get out wordlessly to tether the boat, and the Don follows. Bar the ceaseless lapping of waves, it is silent. There is nothing left on this abandoned Skulk but the mad shark-master's creation and us.

"Come on," says the Don. "Nothing to be afraid of, if it's what you said."

I refrain from asking for that in writing. Instead I get out of the boat and start along the half-sunk jetty ahead of him, leading the way.

"It's intriguing stuff, all this about the power of memory," says the Don behind me, holding up the sheaf of papers as we shuffle carefully along. "Do you credit it at all?"

I wonder if this is a chance to prove myself useful. Perhaps it is a tactic to keep me talking so I cannot plan an escape. To either end it behooves me to talk, because I can plan at the same time.

"I may," I say. "It chimes with some religious theories, that consciousness is more of a great flame than a million tiny little flames, and we're all just parts of the whole, experiencing itself."

The Don grunts, and we turn off the jetty and start down the wooden side of the shark arena. "I've heard of that. Go on."

I think on it some more, the ideas building latently since I realized Mr. Ruin ran a Lag on me without an EMR. "Well, those theories suggest there are actually invisible bonds between all of us. More than bonds really, because we're all actually pieces of the same thing, like radios tuning in on a specific frequency to this grand consciousness bandwidth."

Don Zachary laughs. "I ain't no radio, son."

I ignore him. "Add to that, some people think that at the core of the brain, where no Soul Jacker has ever successfully jacked before, there's a kind of bridge that can reach across to every other mind, like a back door through the bandwidth. Some say there's enormous power there, if we could just reach it."

The Don grunts again, and I don't say any more. We arrive at the ladder leading up to the shark arena. One of the Don's men shoulders in front of me and starts up, leaving me with the Don and the other two. Another of them pulls his gun and points it at my head.

"Precautions," the Don says.

The guy above reaches the top and his footsteps thump over the wood. There's tense silence for a few minutes, then he's back leaning over the edge.

"He's here. In the suit, everything."

The Don gestures for me to climb, and I do, and with every rung up a new plan presents itself. I could simply ride it out and hope the Don will let me go, but that seems unlikely. I could try to overpower the one bodyguard at the top, but he'll probably be standing a ways back with his gun on me, ruling that out.

I wonder if I should risk the bullets. Another plan would be to wait until we're all up close and studying his son, then dive into the froth of the arena. If they don't shoot me mid-dive, escape might be possible, though I'd probably just drown before I swam out from under the Skulk. I reflect sourly on that. Even if I did manage to swim my way out, I'd only pop up a few feet away by the sunken jetty, where they could pick me off like a fish in a barrel.

There's no good plan.

I reach the top of the ladder and get to my feet. As expected, the bodyguard is standing a good distance off in the shadow of the arena, a stray fleck of sunlight glinting off the barrel of his gun.

"Come on in," he says.

I do, and he shuffles backward carefully, keeping his distance. Inside everything is just as I remember it; Napoleon down by the arena, his two-cornered hat slack across his face, his tunic open where I popped out the folder.

I wonder if I am about to go to my death just as he did. Will I perform the pantomime and get into my coffin-suit, on the infinitesimal chance that the Don might let me live? That's getting harder to believe by the second. There's never a cost to killing in the Skulks, but in this abandoned arena so far from everything else, that lack of cost is a palpable thickness in the air, pressing in on me like the drink and madness must have pressed in on the arena's suicidal owner.

I walk down the rotten stands and circle the Don's dead son. Oddly he doesn't look as fat as he was in my memory.

"Scene of the crime," says the Don, emerging at the top of the stands, in the door's oblong of daylight. "How do you feel, Ritry Goligh?"

I don't think it's good that he's using my full name. Like an obituary. "Hungover," I say.

He cackles and starts down the steps.

"So this is my boy," he says, pointing at the corpse in Napoleonic clothing. "I suppose I should be glad it's not in public."

This cements my suspicion: I am certainly going to die here. The Don can't afford to let any sign of weakness get out, even if he believes me about Mr. Ruin, and the murder of one of his own sons can have no living witness. In five seconds I am going to dive for the arena.

Four.

Until then every outward sign I give will be normal with no emotional wind-up at all, a Jacker's particular skill.

Three, two.

One.

Then Napoleon sits up. His hat falls away off, and in the second before the air gets thick with confusion and impossible electromagentism, I see that it is not actually the Don's ugly son, but Mr. Ruin.

The thugs to either side of me drop instantly, as if all their bones have just gone to jelly, like they've been Lagged standing up. I feel the EMR soup rushing beneath the air as it happens, a powerful and throbbing sensation like I'm about to make a jack and the magnets are thumping up around me, only there are no magnets and this is like no jack I ever made before. This is destructive, filling my mind with unseen possibilities.

CRACK

CRACK CRACK

I can't focus. Gun smoke clouds the arena. The Don is hunkered behind a row of seats with his one remaining thug and they're shooting at us.

Ruin's white teeth glint at me in a wide grin, then he nods toward the third thug, who drops on cue. I feel the shift in my Soul or some part of it, like a memory swallowed by the Lag. I'm staring, almost frozen, but now Ruin is moving. He walks up the stands with preternatural grace to stand over Don Zachary, who's now on his knees. I have never seen the Don kneel to another man. Ruin points a finger at the ugly old man's face, and I think in any minute I'm going to feel that strange sense of Lagging dislocation again, but it doesn't come.

Instead Mr. Ruin plucks the folder from the Don's hand. "I believe this belongs to me," he says.

The Don does nothing, just stares as Ruin walks elegantly back down the stands and puts the folder in my hand. He looks at me with eyes so dark I feel like I'm looking into the empty void of space.

"I promised you something to want, Ritry," he says, and taps the folder once with his finger. He then points at the prone Don Zachary. "And here's a reason to run. There's really nothing keeping you in your sad little life."

I open my mouth to say something, but abruptly he's gone, like the record on a turntable skipped. One instant he was there, the next he wasn't, and the EMR-like feeling is stronger than ever.

Lagged again.

Now Don Zachary is shouting and shooting.

CRACK

CRACK

CRACK

I don't think; I run, around the front of the foamy arena and toward the exit. A bullet grazes my shoulder and the pain slices like a syringe in the eye.

CRACK

CRACK

CRACK

I jump over one of the fallen thugs; his eyes are open and full of tears, and I can't help but think of Mei-An on the EMR tray, just chum to the Lag. I snatch my node from his pocket and sprint up the tiered seating chased my gunfire, through the door and into the light where I jump to the jetty below.

My ankle crunches with the landing, but the jetty has some give and the damage can't be too bad. I catch my balance and run on at a hopping limp along the pier toward the speedboat.

CRACK

The Don fires at me from the ladder top and chips spit from a wooden pole nearby, then I leap into the boat. I pull the mooring line loose and while the Don shouts something about nails and my manhood, I rev the engine and tear out of there.

With the wheel in one hand and the stolen node in the other I dial Carrolla, but there is no answer. I can only hope he's in surgery, not already twelve foot deep and drifting amongst the velour of a world long gone. Perhaps I'll never know either way.

The ring clicks to message and I shout into the mouthpiece.

"Get the hell out of the Skulks, Carrolla. Don Zachary's going to kill you, me, whoever he can. Don't stop to raid the jack-site, forget your bar, just pay for passage over the wall and start again in Calico. Just get out." I pause a second, then add a final message. "I'm sorry."

After that I toss the node in the water and race on over the open ocean, bearing for the only place I can think of, and the last place anyone could hope to find me: the lost wreck of the godships.

ME

E. DEATHGATE

We all stare into the candlebomb smoke seeking answers from the freshly-blown hole in the Solid Core, but at this angle there's nothing to see.

"Was that a man?" Ray's voice comes through on blood-mic.

"On a horse," I add.

Nobody speaks further, as we all contemplate what that might mean.

I fire my grapnel before Doe can protest; it's not really the captain's role to dive into the breach, but I can't risk any of the others.

Superheated air buffets me as I swing toward the hole, blurring my HUD. The others clamor protests on blood-mic but I fade them down. I need to focus, because there was something familiar about that man on a horse. It rings a bell in my mind that I didn't know was there. I think the word 'Napoleon', but it doesn't mean anything yet.

I swing up to the gamma-clamp near the gate; the metal around the blast zone has blown outward in jagged triangular chunks, curled back like the petals of some blooming fractal flower.

I fire a traverse wire across the breach and slide between two of the spiky metal outcroppings, coming to a halt directly beneath the blast hole. Only darkness hangs above me; a shaft rising up so black it seems to repel the magma light. There could be a whole world up there, but I can see none of it. I cycle my HUD through the infras and ultras, sonar, radiation and chemical-spec wavelengths but none of it peels away the dark.

"I'm going up."

My grapnel shoots into the darkness and locks onto something two hundred yards in. I work the tracer to slide me up, powering on the whitelights in my suit, and rise like a glowbug up the throat of some giant sleeping beast. Beyond the immediate blast zone the walls either side turn smooth.

"It is an entrance," I say over blood-mic. "The door must have been sealed over but there's a vertical shaft behind it."

As I rise more carvings of silvery foot-high letters appear in the walls, sparkling in my whitelight, many of them crisscrossing one another. "There's writing everywhere."

Doe's voice comes to me as a crackle, bitten at by static. "..areful now, there's …. Can you …. do they say?"

"I can't read them," I answer, "but they look like a hundred different tongues, not just Gaullic. I recognize some proto-Rusk, Afri-Jarvanese, Meso-Angli, Esperant. It's everywhere. I think I'm coming to the inner edge."

Her response is a hiss, but I'm hardly listening as I emerge up from darkness through a field of scraggly grass to see trees, a forest, and a vast space stretching away. I bring the tracer to a halt halfway toward a sheer black ceiling where the grapnel clamped, and hang there like a chandelier in the middle of the space, my whitelights illuminating a battlefield.

There are dead and dying bodies everywhere; scattered amongst the trees, hanging from branches, heaped in piles around dugout furrows in the dirt. I look from one to the next in the search beam of my lights; some dressed in the white tights and blue tunic of the man on the horse, some in rough red greatcoats; all with ancient rifles nearby, all bloodied and filthy and completely still.

None of them move. The whole landscape is deathly still. A man with his leg blown off screams at the edge of a bomb crater, silently and unmoving. A man stares down at his steaming entrails, tangled in the bayonet blade of his enemy and completely frozen. Its unreal.

Further afield there are cottages with their yellow thatch on fire, though the flames don't move at all. There's a brook that doesn't run, and a watermill that doesn't turn. There are kicking gray horses lying in troughs of bloody mud, caught in the instant, and a wooden cart in mid-explosion with a cannon ball hovering uncannily in its fragmented midst. Everywhere bodies lie in the heated embrace of static battle. The flash of their polished brass buttons wink at me like a star-field.

My mind warps to take it in. I feel dizzy and ill, like I'm looking at the world through a distorting periscope prism.

"What do you see, Me?"

It takes me a moment to recognize Doe's voice. I'm sweating. I don't like this; it's worse than being outside, but it must be the way forward. I click back my visor because I need some air, but it's hardly air at all; there is no stink of burning or blood, no green sap from the trees or peat from the dirt. The air is sterile and empty.

"You'll have to come up," I say into blood-mic.

Soon they are beside me. We stand in a narrow clearing by the lip of the shaft, surrounded by frozen dead bodies. A cluster of our lights hang from the ceiling overhead, casting this strange world in a monochrome wash of grays.

Ray sucks in a sharp, angry breath. "What kind of bullshit is this?" he asks.

Far trembles in the holster at his side.

"It looks like a giant's playset," Doe says. "A toy battle. What do you make of it, Me?"

I don't make anything. These soldiers look dead, but the one who fell through the hole was moving. He shouted. We shouldn't feel safe.

"Basecamp is around that tree," I say, taking command. "QCs at the ready, perimeter here." I point in a circle and sling the overmap to their HUD visors. "Far in the middle with So and La working on mapping and materials analysis; see if you can figure out what's going on here. Doe and Ray, we start clearing the bodies."

So and La jolt into action, unsnapping bits of equipment from their suits. I escort Far to the tree, then join Ray and Doe with their QCs drawn, shifting the frozen bodies. Ray lifts the first by the arm; a man clutching a chest wound. His whole body moves as Ray lifts, with no give in the limbs.

"Rigor mortis?" I ask.

Ray grunts. "Not that. He's hard all over. Let's try…" He pops a knife from its waist sheath and digs it into the dead man's exposed throat, but only the tip of the blade enters, chewing out a tiny chip of some hard material. Ray picks the blue chip up and rubs it between his fingers.

"Some kind of plastic," he says.

There's nothing I can say to that. "Analyze it please, La," I say. She takes the chip and unclips more equipment from her suit.

"It's all fake," Doe says as we clear more bodies; tossing them beyond the perimeter. They aren't too heavy, certainly not with the suit exo-motors engaged. We're on a command blood-mic channel now, for just the three of us. "There's no texture on their skin. The pattern of veins is painted on."

She slings a closeup image to my visor. It redoubles the sick feeling.

Ray picks up one of the soldiers' old wooden rifles and sights down the barrel. "This looks real enough." He points it away from us and pulls the trigger, but there's only a metallic click. "Dud," he says.

"Is there something about this in the mission pack?" Doe asks.

I turn to her. She's right, with any immediate threat handled we need to dig into the mission itself, but I don't want to do it over blood-mic, through the HUDs. I can see her eyes through the visor, and her flat expression, but that's not enough for the conversation we need to have, where one of us might be a traitor. I need to do this without the HUDs on.

"We're reconnoitering," I say on the open line, then gesture to Ray and Doe to follow as I start into the woods.

There are dead bodies everywhere inside, lying in darkness until our whitelights come near. I have to push between the tree branches in places, their leaves flexing and bending stiffly. I pluck a leaf as I go and study its surface. It has a waxy sheen and is completely symmetrical. I tear it cleanly down the middle. The vein-lines on its surface do not continue through the middle, as if they were printed on.

Nothing seems real. I lead us to a clearing ringed with the bodies of red and blue soldiers and several cannon, fringed with the watermill I spotted from the grapnel. A puff of black smoke hangs in the air above the chimney, like a thin ball of black wool.

There is no way inside the building, only a wood-effect doorway frame with a shallow alcove; just one more disconcerting detail. There I stop and take off my HUD, waiting for the others to do the same.

They do. I ready the speech I've been composing in my mind.

"We're in this together," I say, "we're a chord."

"Of course," says Ray.

"Yes," says Doe.

"But we don't know who we are, not really." I pause and look at them, seeking something in their eyes. "We have a feeling only. We're a chord, but we don't remember each other more than a vague sensation. I believe I'm the captain and you seem to believe it too, but how do you know?"

Ray points at my suit. "You've got the insignia."

I look down at the complex yellow design on my chest, like a maze. I'd forgotten about it. "And how do you know what this means?"

"Like you say, it's just a feeling," says Doe.

I nod, considering. "You're my lieutenants, and I feel I can trust you both, but I don't know if I can trust that feeling. It seems like you're closer to me somehow. As for So and La, I don't have that same feeling. Before I say anything more though, I want to know what you think."

"They're on the other side of Far," says Ray.

I look at his sharp, green eyes. He looks honest. "What does that mean?"

He shrugs. "In the forge-pods they were on the other side of Far, and Far's a weird kid. Like a kind of bridge."

I think back to those first moments in the sublavic corridor as I stumbled out of the forge fire, looking sideways at Doe, then Ray and Far with the others beyond.

"Understood. Doe?"

She shrugs. "They seem loyal to me. Maybe they're distant, but so was Ti, and she died to save us. Why does it matter?"

I look at Ray and he looks at me.

"It was the first page of the mission book," I say. "It said, 'Don't read this out loud. One of your chord will kill you all.'"

She takes a second. "So that's why you didn't read it. I thought that was strange. And you believe it?"

"I don't know. I have to be careful." I pull out the mission pack.

"What's Ritry Goligh?" Doe asks, looking at the title.

"We don't know," Ray chimes in. "Do you?"

Doe shakes her head. "A feeling, maybe."

"OK," I say, and flip to the blank first page.

"T-minus one," says Ray.

"Pay attention." I slip a finger under the flap of the next page. "The ink fades in seconds. Ready?" They nod and I turn it.

It's a mission brief page with three words in a large font, each of which begin to fade at once.

SAVE RITRY GOLIGH

That's all. I scour the page as the ink lightens away but there is nothing else. I look to Ray and Doe.

"There he is again," Ray says.

"How is that a mission objective?" Doe asks. "We don't know this person."

I grunt, and edge my finger under the next page. "Ready?" I ask. They nod and I flip it, and three things happen at once.

One, strident and impossible to ignore, is the scream from the forest. I know at once it is Far, and he is terrified.

Two, the sharp crack of rifle fire rings out, and the bright nimbus of light from the whitelight cluster we hung over the hole is extinguished, plunging us into a swaddling darkness lit only by our suit lights.

Three, I see the fading writing in the mission pack, echoing the scream back at me.

SAVE FAR

F. MUSKETS

Ray is first to start running back around the cottage, bolting on his HUD as he goes, bringing up his pistol and QC rifle. Doe and I sprint after him as Far in the distance screams again.

"What's happening?" I shout through blood-mic, "So, La, report," but I get only static back, mingled with Ray's heavy breathing.

Ray hits the tree line and dissolves amongst the thick plastic foliage, with Doe and me right behind. It's hard to see anything beyond the nearest branches, reflecting my suit lights harshly back at me, so I flash through the ultraviolet range in my HUD until I fall upon infrared, and the view phases into heat-vision tones of cool purple and green.

On that plain backdrop Ray is a hot orange silhouette, driving forward through cold blue brush. In the clearing ahead the hot shapes of So, La and Far are huddled together, surrounded by a group of advancing blue and purple figures.

My blood runs cold, as either So or La falls to the ground beneath the encircling horde. The other figure is standing and shooting QC particles in waves, each a tiny red blip on the screen.

"They're waking up!" Doe shouts on mic, even as I see something purple loom at me out of the trees. I flick back to regular vision to see one of the plastic soldiers striding toward me, his rifle held forward with the bayonet sparkling in my suit lights. His face is normal but for the mouth, which is a black and chomping gash stretching down into his neck. There's blood stained from a bandaged wound in his head and he's almost upon me.

I disassociate him with one blast of the QC, but he doesn't blow apart like he should, he only staggers backward. I follow and drive the haft of my pistol into his solid plastic forehead with a thunk, followed by a suit-enhanced kick that sends him arcing back into the screen of trees.

"The QCs are ineffective," I call on blood-mic as I run on, "use the suit exos."

"Roger that," Ray shouts. Far's scream rings out louder now, then I burst out of the trees into the clearing.

There must be fifty plastic soldiers gathered in a rough circle around my chord. Their backs are to us, red coats and blue tunics intermingling like they've called a truce and are huddling for warmth. They're pressed against a pale red dome rising up in their midst, and I'm thankful that La had the sense to erect the lava shield we brought from the sublavic.

The shield's red surface ripples like a film of oil on water, and I wonder how long the power supply can hold back the plastic soldiers. I start firing QC particles into their mass as fast as the pistol will charge.

"Carve a path and we evac," I call out on blood-mic, "report!"

Ray is already ahead of me and pulling at the soldiers with his hands, tossing them backward. "Carving," he calls back. "Do something about the ones I've cleared."

"Roger that," I answer and stride up to one of them and unload a stream of QCs into its mouth. Even at this range though there is no dissociating effect; if anything its black mouth starts to chomp faster.

Far screams again and I hear the breathy voice of So on blood-mic. "They have La. Get us out of here, Me!"

I hurl the chomping soldier to the side, engaging exos to fling it far into the forest, but a part of me knows it will come back. Ray hurls more from the pack and I catch a few and hurl them further, but it won't be enough; we need another way. Then Doe is by my side and unshouldering the bondless cannon, a heavy chunk of black metal that contains a compressed atomic accelerator.

"Cut a path for Ray," I tell her. "I'll keep them out. Ray, keep doing what you're doing."

Doe nods as she assembles the weapon and sets the tripod braces into the ground. Ray calls a grunting, "Roger," as he hurls more soldiers aside.

I pull out my grapnel and fire one hook into the nearest tree. It catches and I pull the line taut, then start to run, weaving around and between the soldiers as they rise back to their feet and make for Ray. They chomp their teeth at me and grab at my arms and legs but I'm too fast, wrapping each one in the cord like a spider wrapping flies in its web.

I enfold ten, perhaps fifteen before their collective drag begins to pull me with them. I cut and re-head the elasteel rope end then fire it back to the same tree with an automatic tracer. The hook locks in and begins to wind, and the entangled soldiers are jerked off their feet and dragged toward it, bundled tight to the tree.

I turn to Doe and see she's set behind the cannon, aimed squarely at Ray's back buried three soldiers deep into their ranks. "We're coming," I rasp into blood-mic for So and Far, then to Doe I shout, "now."

The percussive shock is nothing next to the recoil, as a golden spray of bondless atoms jets out of the accelerator cannon's funnel end. Doe is knocked flat on her back. The golden mist blasts over the crowd, quickly evaporating as the atoms slip off their sheaths of non-reactive gold and affix to the plastic backs of the soldiers, ripping chunks out of them in instant bond-destruction.

Soldiers stagger, several drop, but not nearly as many as I'd hoped. Ray leaps into the shallow breach, protected by the ion-charge in his suit, and continues hurling bodies backward with his suit exos whining loudly. I follow with another grapnel trap hooked to another tree. I loop more soldiers in webbing until Ray's cleared a path up to the lava shield's edge, and we can just see the black-suited form of La lying underneath their feet.

I fire the grapnel again, my last, and it bundles another batch of soldiers away, but still Ray can't quite reach La's body. She's too entwined amongst the soldiers' feet, and most of his efforts now are spent keeping the tunnel walls he's carved through their ranks from collapsing in on him.

"Help me, Me," he calls, and the fear in his voice startles me.

"Again," I shout to Doe, and dive into the breach as the second atomic blast peel out. The gold sprays like star dust and a few more bodies fall ahead and to either side, dropping across La's prone body.

Ray darts in and snatches her up. "I've got her!" he shouts and starts back. A soldier in a blue tunic grabs at his knee but I drive it off with a firm kick. Together we force our way back down the tunnel as the plastic walls close in.

Doe lets loose another blast with a curse, just enough to ease us free of their grasping arms. "It's doing less each time," she grunts, as the wall of bodies reseals. Far's cries have gotten weaker and the whuff of So's QC pistol cuts only intermittently through the buzz of the lava shield.

We lurch to a stop beside Doe, and Ray drops La at our side. I can see at once that she's in hideous shape. There are bayonet gouges in her midriff through which blood has leaked, though there's no way any normal blade could have gotten through the armor. There's a deeply cracked pockmark in her shoulder where a musket ball must have torn it away, like an impact crater, impossible for any normal projectile to do.

"It's the … gravometric … bonds," La gulps, as Doe leans over her prone body and runs her fingers across the resealed wound. She looks up at me desperately, blood spilling like engine oil from her lips. "They're just …more solid … than us."

"Do something!" comes So's cry through blood-mic, and I turn to see the top arc of the lava shield sputtering. This too is impossible, something bayonets and rifle fire should not be able to achieve in a million years, but it's happening before my eyes.

More solid than we are. An idea comes and I leap on it.

I toss my QC to the floor and scour the fake grass until I spot a fallen musket. Three steps and I pick it up, then I'm at the soldier wall and driving the bayonet into the back of the nearest soldier.

It goes in like I'm carving wet clay, deep in past the blade's edge and halfway up the rifle barrel to spike out of the soldier's front and stab into the one in front.

They both give a sigh, their chomping jaws stop, and they drop. I let go of the buried musket as they drag it down with them, staring for a moment in disbelief. Then I snatch both the muskets from their hands and toss the extra one to Ray, already at my side.

"Doe, keep the cannon coming," I shout, "So get yourself a musket and use it, Ray, it's you and me out here."

He nods, gold dust envelops us like a cloak, and side by side we stab a path through the soldiers, dropping them sighing to the ground and stepping on their fallen bodies. For long desperate minutes stabbing and slashing are all I do, through their backs and heads, across chests and faces. I stab them two and three at a time like skewered kebabs, slice them like meatloaf portions, even as the flickering red shield ahead sputters, fades and dies.

We burst through the final rank of soldiers and into the inner circle seconds after the shield cracks. So is there with a musket in her hand and fierce determination written over the desperation. Far is curled up with his hands over his eyes at the tree's base and all around us are the pressing ranks of the soldiers, advancing. Still there are too many and I know that they'll soon overwhelm us, like ants swarming a scorpion.

Then So cranks one of the muskets and points it at the nearest soldier, depresses the trigger, and-

CRACK

The musket ball shears through the model soldiers like the QC should have, felling a handful in a straight line. She cranks it again, takes aim and nods at me. Better than bayonets.

"Get a cannon, Doe," I call over blood-mic. "A real cannon."

So's next shot cracks out and a half dozen more bodies fall and don't get up. I crank my own musket just like So, aim it at the nearest bulge in the mass of pressing plastic and fire. Soldiers tumble all in a line.

Soon Ray, So and I are back-to-back in a triangle, all shooting, adrenaline buoying us on as we scythe straight lines through the soldiers, stepping in to drive our bayonets through any stragglers. Their numbers never seem to end though, and I'm tiring fast, then-

BOOM

The cannon-shot shakes the air like thunder, and abruptly half of the soldiers are blown to smithereens. A great gap appears in their ranks, and I see Doe through it with a fuse in her hand and a cannon at her side.

"Amazing," she says on blood-mic.

We shoot into the remaining half of soldiers until Doe levels most of them with another blast. We pick off the remnants with bayonets; a massacre with no screams or blood.

Afterward there is a curious absence of sound, beyond the ragged breathing of our chord and Far's quiet sobbing. I am sweat-slicked and exhausted, but the battle is over. We won.

I turn, taking in the scene. Far is still huddled by the tree, So, Ray and Doe have their HUDs off and are all steaming. So has a wild, fractured look in her eyes. Around us there is a mandala of dead plastic bodies like the layers of a Molten Core. Occasionally one of their black mouths chomps at the air.

"Did we kill them all?" comes Ray's voice.

A long eerie moment passes as we sweep the trees around us, waiting for more to emerge, but none do.

The chord look to me. I am the captain, and my job is to lead, so I blink away the uncertainty and start giving orders.

"Ray, help Far. Doe, walk a patrol. Everybody take your shock-jacks." I hit the button for a shock-jack myself, releasing a stored flow of my own body's soothing chemicals, designed to counteract the numbing, sickening after-effects of combat. At once I feel the impact, becoming more relaxed and attuned to the world. My sense of smell returns and the fog in my hearing clears.

The chord follow my orders, and Ray goes to Far while Doe lifts a musket and starts for the tree-line perimeter, leaving only So.

I turn to her. The wild look is still in her eyes. She was here when they seized La and dragged her underfoot. I walk over and take her by the hand, and I lead her to Doe is working frantically to save La.

Have I lost another tone in the chord already?

G. LA

Doe does everything she can.

Their suits and systems are linked, so Doe can give whatever blood, plasma and shock-jacks La might need, but as the seconds pass she draws less and less. Soon she is barely breathing, looking up at us and mouthing sounds none of us can make out. The suit knows there is no benefit to any further fluid transfer, because she is too far gone.

Tears stream from So's eyes as the last breath wheezes out of La's lips.

Then La is dead. Another chord member lost.

"Rest," I say gently to So, "there was nothing you could do."

She doesn't listen. Instead she starts working at the clasps of La's armor, unlatching them one by one. I lay a hand on hers and say, "We don't have to do this now," but she only pulls away and keeps going.

I let go. It's no time to pull rank. Instead I help, popping clasps down La's right side, and we lift off her chest-plate together.

Her innards spill out onto the ground like hot soup. They have been liquefied, as though scrambled by a QC particle. I can see clear through to the bone-white shards of her spine, embedded in the inner black casement of the suit. The hot smell of burned blood rises from the mess trickling through the fake grass around our knees, and So turns pale.

I reach to her again but again she pulls away, her eyes hot and wet.

"How could this happen?" she whispers. "How could bayonets do this, Me?"

I have nothing to say, and this plainly scares her worse. So is normally quiet and restrained, hidden behind the twins, but now both of the twins are dead. She drops La's casement and lurches to her feet.

"So," I call after her, but she staggers away. I watch as she moves amongst the dead model soldiers, plunging her musket bayonet through their chests and heads like it's a sharp cane sinking into cheese.

Far is looking at me. He's squatted by the tree still, his eyes red-rimmed. I try to smile but he only turns away.

SAVE FAR

The mission pack said it, but I don't understand.

I turn on blood-mic to the remains of my chord. "La is dead. I'm sorry for it. The bayonets disrupted her like a QC. Only the suit was holding her together." A pause. "Report."

Another pause holds as the others silently acknowledge this, then Doe's voice comes in, settled and calm, the shock-jack doing its job. "Nothing. There's nothing moving out here Me, just like it was before."

I watch So; on her knees now and sawing at a soldier's neck. I flip blood-mic to my lieutenants. "Talk to me about what all that was."

"Defenses," Doe says sharply. "Something doesn't want us going any deeper."

"Agreed," says Ray. "There's something in the air here, something not right. Maybe it's those bonds La was talking about. We're not supposed to be here."

I watch as So cuts through a soldier's neck and lifts the head clear, dropping it to the side. She's frenzied; out of control. It's this place.

"Nothing's bonded correctly," Doe goes on. "The longer we stay here, the worse it'll get."

They're both right. We are not meant to be here, and we need to get this mission done as soon as possible. I pull out the pack and flip to the next page.

INFLITRATE THE INNER MAZE

Beneath it there is a vaguely familiar schematic diagram, all lines and circles, which begins to fade at once. I catch a freeze-frame of it in my HUD then sling it to the others. Ray comes back to me quickly.

"It's the design on your chest, Me. It's your insignia."

I look down at the circular symbol printed bright yellow on my uniform front, and it does seem to match. I wonder what that might mean.

I bring up the image in my HUD: a series of intricate concentric circles cut through with yellow oblongs, triangles and smaller circles, lined up like transistors on a circuit board.

"It's a map," says Doe.

The image slings back from her with a flashing red dot added, staked out to the right of the only entrance in the outer circle. "That's us," Doe says, "next to the Deathgate."

I track the next ring in until it also breaks, on the exact opposite side of the sphere. I flip to the next page in the pack, but it's empty. Every page after that is empty, like some kind of joke.

We're not supposed to be here. We can't go back.

"We're moving now," I say sharply. "Ray, get Far and strip any equipment we might need from La's suit. Doe, figure some way to bring that cannon with us. Mount it to your suit if you can. I'll deal with So."

They Roger it and start moving.

I go to So, still at her grisly work. I watch as she cuts off heads and stacks them into small heaps.

"We're going to bury La," I say.

She slices through the current soldier's last stretch of neck, drops the head on her pile and turns to me. She's not crying any more. She's empty.

"Tell me this is worth it, Me," she says. "Tell me something."

I look into her black eyes and see the pain of this loss taking root, along with a kind of madness. Both La and Ti is too much for her, and this place is biting into her already.

"It's worth it," I say, and pray to Ritry Goligh that I'm telling her the truth. "Believe in the chord, So. It is worth it."

She stares at me a long moment, then drops the musket to the ground. "I'll kill you if you're lying."

I nod. I'll welcome death at her hand, if I'm lying. "Let's bury La first."

She bites her lip and nods.

I rewrap La's suit. Doe and Ray gather in and Ray says a few words, though I'm sure he knows no more about La than I, or Doe, or even So herself. She was just another one of us, lost.

We carry her together to the drop; she's so light. We clip her body into a traverse wire and reel it out until she's hanging beside the whitelight cluster above the open Deathgate. I say a silent thank you then cut the clasp.

La's body falls down through the black shaft toward the lava. I lean over to watch as she tumbles in the hot updrafts, growing smaller. Soon she is the size of a dropped pebble, then a black speck of grit, then finally an infinitesimal spark in the Molten Core far below.

"She's with her sister now," Doe says.

So goes to Far and wraps her arm around him, pushing her face into the side of his head. For some reason this makes me want to cry too.

Two down, five to go.

H. MAZE

We leave So behind.

I know it may be a death sentence, but there is no choice. She is our expert in mapping, and already she's losing her mind. I need her as clear-headed as possible, and I don't think she can take another level deeper in.

She accepts this with a sigh. "I'll die."

"We're coming back," I promise her, though I know it may be a lie. "We're a chord. You be strong for us and we'll be strong for you."

"I'm already gone, Me," she says, then stands and points. "I'll put telemetry receivers here and here. I'll build your map."

I resist saying more. I want to, but there's nothing to say, and every second counts now. She drifts away amongst her heaped heads, setting up equipment.

Ray's hand comes on my shoulder. Doe stands beside me, the huge cannon now mounted on her left shoulder.

"We have to go," she says.

I nod.

I shoot my grapnel and lead us to the plain black ceiling. Directly above the Deathgate Doe rigs a second candlebomb, and triggers the blast. Nothing falls out this time; there's hardly even any smoke. I look back to So a final time, moving amongst her severed heads like a memory already. Another tone in the chord lost to save the whole, to save Ritry Goligh, then I shoot a grapnel up through the ruptured gap and ascend into-

-darkness.

I feel dizzy and sick. Soemthing just happened but I don't know what, like I pushed through a soap bubble and the world popped around me. The tracers halt as I hit a yielding ceiling, and my visor is dark; the suit has powered down. I give the command to restart and my suit lights fire up, illuminating a twisting, organic array of five tunnels stretching away form me.

I turn and stare. The tunnels are roughly circular in cross-section, a mottled pink with spidery purple lines, like I've ascended into the veins of a giant body. The tunnels flex and shift in time to a distant thumping pulse, like blood pumping from a great heart.

thump thump

thump thump

But it's not blood. I feel it in the vibrations, like I can feel the churn of the Molten Core. Something is coming.

"Me, come in, answer me now!"

The voice in my HUD slaps me alert and I switch on blood-mic. "I'm here, Doe, what is it?"

The relief in her voice is palpable. "Oh, thank Goligh. Me, what happened? Where did you go?"

"I'm inside," I answer, slinging my feed of the pulsing tunnels. "What happened?"

"What happened? You've been out of contact for ten minutes."

I check my suit feeds, but the internal clock has reset. Ten minutes? "It felt like seconds to me., I-"

"What the hell is that?" Ray interrupts. "What are we looking at, Me?"

"Tunnels," I say. "Organic. Get up here."

"Roger," says Doe, "inbound."

The signal cuts, and I wait for two more grapnels lines to shoot into the ceiling beside me, but they don't come. Time lag, I think.

thump thump

thump thump

I unharness and drop onto the tunnel surface; it bows beneath my weight, the meat of the floor indenting under my feet.

"Doe, Ray," I bark into blood-mic. "So?"

No answer comes.

I switch on the suit's telemetry aerials and they start transmitting the sonar of this strange, undulating place back to So. Minutes pass, and still no grapnels appear. I look down the hole but there is nothing to see, only a well of inky darkness.

thump thump

thump thump

The sound grows louder. The vein-tunnels throb harder.

So's voice comes back.

"Me?"

She sounds faint and whispery, like a ghost.

"So, can you hear me? Come in, So."

After a five-second delay of hazy white noise, she answers. "I have you, Me. Do you have me?"

She sounds so plaintive. "I do. So, I'm sending telemetries, are you receiving?"

"Yes. Me, did you send Ti here?"

A chill steals over my heart. For a second I think I must have misheard her. "Come again, So, did you say Ti?"

"She's here," So answers, her tone sing-songy and frail. "She's just looking at me."

My throat seizes up. "That's not possible, So. Ti's dead."

"Oh. She's just staring. What should I tell her?"

There are no words. I gulp. "So, do you see Ray and Doe?"

"Ray and Doe? No. They went up."

They went up. Of course they did; there's some kind of time lag. I focus.

"So, do you have a map for me?"

"A map," she muses. I picture her floating like flotsam on a slow tide. "Yes. Ti, what do you think of this? Are my calculations correct?"

"Send it to me," I manage, choked out through my tight throat. "Don't worry about Ti."

"Sending," So murmurs. The line crackles, then an image slings into my HUD; a wireframe schematic of a multi-shelled sphere riddled with passageways and odd little nodules that must be rooms. A red dot flashes in the outermost layer.

"And the route?"

"La's here now too," So whispers. She sounds like a child version of herself. "They're holding hands, Me. They want me to come with them."

"Don't go with them!" I snap. "So, I need you. The rest of the chord needs you. Stay with me!"

A long pause follows. "They're upset with me. They're eating the heads. Me, I don't want to eat the heads."

"Then don't. Give me the route, So."

"Yes. It's a rotational maze, Me," she explains. "I took the flat map on your chest and spun it to a globe. It matches what you see around you. Here." A red line appears like a long worm folded through the Core, leading to the center. "Don't step off it. I can't predict what would happen if you stray."

"We won't, I promise, now So-"

"They're calling, Me, we'll throw bodies down the shaft. Last one to bed's a sore loser!"

"So!" I call, "stop, that's an order."

She kills the blood-mic connection. I blink away the map, sweating in the warm air of the tunnel, just as two grapnels shoot up through the blast-hole and dig into the pulsing roof. Doe, Ray and Far follow.

"Holy shit," Ray says, watching the tunnels contort as a heavy pulse hits.

thump thump

"There was a time lag coming up," I say, guiding them on to the fleshy floor. Ray looks at his feet in disgust as they sink in, while Doe takes in the tunnels silently. There are strange weals marking Far's face and neck, but there is no time to deal with that now. "I used the time to reach out to So, and she has a route."

"Good," says Doe, "we need to move right now."

Another pulse comes and almost knocks me from my feet.

thump thump

Doe points down one of the tunnels, where the walls are distending; bulging inward to meet in the middle. Orders catch in my throat as the walls conjoin then split like an over-ripe peach. The torn tunnel edges turn outside in to form a sucking black mouth at the head of a worm-like body that begins to slithers back along itself, toward us.

I stare in horror.

thump thump

Its lips smack in time with the hard rhythm of some strange Soul's heartbeat, peeling the tunnel walls round into itself like a tube inside a tube, and finally I get the word out of my frozen throat.

"Run!"

I lead us in a mad sprint left and right down a branching network of heaving tunnels that sway with their own life. Far is screaming again on blood-mic, drowning out everything else. I scan So's map in my HUD for shelter as I take a sharp left into what looks like the ventricle of a heart, followed by an inclined left down into a sludgy low-ceilinged cave.

"Hurry, Me!" Doe shouts over Far's wailing.

I chance a look back; the snake-worm thing is gaining on us. I find what looks to be a triangular room just ahead and-

thump thump

The pulse grows thunderous and knocks me off my feet. A gush of viscous fluid washes over me, carrying the gnashing worm on a tide, and I slip, try to pull myself up on the wall but there is no purchase to be gained.

"Stay down," comes Doe's shout, then-

BOOM

I feel the cannon ball rush over my head like a swooping crull, skidding off the intestinal walls to impact solidly against the worm's face. It tears a gout of white away, thick blood spumes out and the pulse goes haywire.

thump thump

thump thump

Doe fires again.

BOOM

Then Ray hoists me up and I'm in the lead again, running along So's route and directly toward another gnashing worm's mouth.

The route's cut off! I shoulder my musket and fire a continuous stream of lead balls at the smacking lips, peppering it with purple weals that spit dark blood, even as I spin So's sphere in my HUD searching for another place to hide.

I find a circular module off to the right, off the route, but I don't see any choice now. Doe's cannonballs aren't stopping them.

thump thump

BOOM

Doe wins us precious seconds and I lead us off the route to the palpitating mass of wall where the door should be. I stab my musket into the glistening flesh and slice it down like I'm undoing a zip, releasing a shower of slime.

Ray drives his bayonet in beside me and zips in parallel as the worms thump toward us with Doe just ahead. I force the gouge open to reveal a dank circular room, and Doe dives through the gap.

"Go," I shout, and Ray follows her through, then the lips are upon me and I finally grasp what they are; lethal cousins to the Lag. At once I know what I have to do, and toss the memory of Ti into them like a grenade.

It explodes and the mouths rupture in a spray of pink mist. I dive through the gap and into the circular chamber beyond, where Ray slams a rusted metal hatch closed.

I pant, and Doe lifts me to my feet.

It's a round and rusted metal room, and every surface is stamped with a stippled pattern of initials.

RG

I snort. Ritry Goligh.

thump thump

thump thump

The rusted hatch bucks inward; Ray leans his weight against it without needing to be told. The worms are coming. I don't know what there is to say, as various unerstandings flood through my mind; I just threw something at the Lag, some memory of myself, but I don't know what it was.

The hole it made aches inside, though, like I gave up part of myself.

"Ti," Far says. He's not screaming anymore. I look at him, trying to frame words around this concept I barely understand. I don't know what that word means; then it is gone. I can't even remember what he said. Memories are weapons, and when they're gone they're gone.

I blink, and scan the room again, and finally see the book.

It is enormous, bound in red leather and filling the space like a shock-attack lowboat. The title is written across its front in embossed gold.

VEN

But who is Ven? I do not know; I can't remember.

The lips smack at the door behind us, the thump thump pulse burrs through the tin floor, and now I know just what to do. If memory is a weapon, we need to gear up. I open the book and start to read.

RITRY GOLIGH

9. GODSHIPS

It takes four hours before the first of the godships comes into sight. They are a dirty brown smudge on the clay-gray horizon, rusted hulls split like rotten bananas on a garbage patch of dark rock, barely emerging above the waves.

I try to count them, but the bucking of the speedboat against the rough water prevents me. There have to be dozens; maybe the whole fleet. I see half a hull sticking up at a diagonal here, a tilted glimpse of white-above decks there, a bulbous prow jutting proudly up like a long nose. It's a vast ocean graveyard, and the closer I get the bigger they are.

I shake my head to clear it, and am greeted by the drilling pain of my Arcloberry hangover. A thousand brain cells dead with every sip. My shoulder stings in the salt wind where Don Zachary's bullet grazed it, though the cut has long dried over. My stomach throbs where it met his bat.

I need to lie down.

The godships draw closer, looming like brown cliffs, spotted in places with the sheen of intact glass. Several hulls have their backs broken over the rocks, left upturned like drooping brown slugs. There are forecastles skewed at wild angles like dirty wind-blown icicles. There's a gossamer network of cables, threads and walkways strung between them, like spiderwebs shining with winter dew.

The fuel gauge on the speedboat blips. The dial has sunk down below the halfway mark, and I wonder if it'll be enough to take me back to the Skulks.

I choke the engine down beside one of the bigger, more intact ships, so close I can smell the iron stink of its rust and hear the wind whistling through its cracks and broken portholes. It is completely upended in the water, a cragged brown wall of hull leading up to the keel. The rear end has sheared away, perhaps torn by the tsunami that fated it, or one that followed. One of its propellers though remains nearby, wedged like a sparkling star in the rocks and scoured a bright silver by decades of corrosive saltwater.

I can read the ship's name, stenciled in paint almost too faint to make out, upside down toward the underside's bulbous nose.

SAINT AQUINAS OF YLEP

From the proto-Rusk federation. I look around at the others, representatives of all the major nation-states who united in faith before the global tsunamis hit: Afri-Jarva, the Gaullic Federation, Sino-Anglica, the draggled remnants of the Texarchy. All were gathered up by the unstoppable pulse of tsunami waves and dumped here.

The Ylep shows signs of recent habitation. At the top there's a line of slipshod timber walkway bolted into the great ship's keel, leading along to a few tiny huts beaten out of ship's tin, within one of which glimmers a bright reflection.

I recognize the pattern of a Fresnel lens, signifying a lighthouse. We often ported these lenses through the War and dropped them in four-man payloads on strategic rock outcroppings or old oil-rigs, before submersing again. Focused light from the Fresnels was unjammable, with a range of over fifty nautical miles; far enough to get a signal back to our base ships moored at the War line.

There is no sign of any life here now. Perhaps the last wave fifteen years ago cleared them all out. The walkway sags, and the haulage rope hanging down the Ylep's side no longer reaches the water.

"Hello!" I call.

No answer comes, only the lonely echo of my own voice. I lean in to guide the speedboat through a maze of rocks toward the Ylep.

Rounding the great ship's cloven middle, I can clearly see the damage wrought when the rear half was torn away. The hull in cross-section is warped; several decks lower down have been crushed while others have popped too wide. It's like looking at a dollhouse with the front wall open, with all its brickwork and plumbing laid bare; elevator shafts with cars hanging like cans of beans on strings, corridors that are holes leading into darkness, one end of a grand hall where the chandelier lies broken on the floor that was once the roof.

I imagine people from the past moving inside, servants and masters, dancers and lovers, leading their lives. They are thick in the air like ghosts, and perhaps it is the hangover, but I feel the weight of them pressing down upon me.

I nudge the speedboat forward, down a channel in the rock that leads into a berth at the Ylep's base. It grows gloomy as I enter the makeshift garage and bring the speedboat to a halt.

There are other small craft here, two jet-skis and a tug barge resting on a metal platform above the water. There is graffiti on the walls, written in the jagged proto-Rusk alphabet that my old memory implants translate faithfully.

MEN'S HEAD

WOMEN'S HEAD

I kill the engine and step out of the speedboat. The metal harbor is solid, and I scan the walls for a route heading up, finding a sprayed red sign indicating BRIDGE and pointing to stairs.

The stairwell is bright and broad, with regular portholes letting in floods of light. I climb peeling plaster steps that were once the ceiling, my feet clanging loudly on metal, and it gets lighter and breezier as I rise, with the cracked portholes let in sighing sea air. Arrows for the BRIDGE point me upward, while others appear alongside them.

HABITATION

CANTEEN

NETTING

CHAPEL

On the first HABITATION deck landing three flights up I hear something. It sounds like a whisper, or a set of overlapping whispers, perhaps calling my name.

I stop, heart pounding, and listen. Above the low breath of the wind, the drip of water percolating through the ancient decks and the creak of doors swaying on their hinges I can almost make out what the voices are saying.

They are very far off, yet they're all around me still, like bubbles of memory bursting in the lava of a Molten Core. That's not possible though; I'm nowhere near an EMR.

I walk through the stairwell door, beyond which stretches a long upside down hallway. The roof is lined with red and gold carpet, the walls are furnished with white picture rails and paintings of ships at sea, interspersed with dark wooden doors hanging from the ceiling, all marked with upside down numbers. The floor is gray metal lined with gray pipes and the nubs of old light fixtures.

A wave of feeling rises and hits me then, like fountaining data from a living mind; some indistinct emotion I barely recognize but am powerless to repel, a kind of nostalgia for a past I never knew.

The feeling grows and the voices get louder as I advance, swelling over me so I catch fragments of their conversation on the air: talking about how the dinner service went, about that sweet old couple at last night's Waltz for God, about whether Stacy was sleeping with Reg or Clancy. Interspersed are the sounds of voices rising in ecstasy, then in panic, then a deep low grinding as the ship is lifted in the air and flipped like a crull on a griddle.

I shudder and slump against the corridor wall as my legs turn to jelly. What the hell? I feel like I'm high, but this is no fun at all. It's terrifying, like being trapped in a dying mind.

"Jesus, shit," I mutter, trying to get control back. I close my eyes and focus. None of this is real. Did the Don inject me with some kind of hallucinogen?

Gradually the voices quieten, down to a distant tickle in the back of my mind, and another thought strikes me. Mr. Ruin was talking about something like this; the power of memories left behind, and I recognize this distant buzz of foreign minds in the air, like the empty frame of a memory lost to the Lag.

I rub my eyes and walk further down the corridor. "Hello," I call out, though I know no one's here. I throw open the first door and look in on a room filled with junk. There is a large rectangular window cut through the outer hull, illuminating a bed covered in tangled sheets, clothes on the floor, a wooden dresser tipped on its side and assorted toys everywhere.

Whoever squatted here after the ship was wrecked never meant to leave, I realize. They had no time. I think back to the last tsunami warning, when half of the Skulks of proto-Calico were abandoned and empty, when I walked into the old jack-site and claimed it for my own. These squatters must have fled too, with no time to gather their possessions.

I'm too hungry and hungover to think clearly. I head back to the stairwell and climb until I find the floor for CANTEEN. It's a large hall with open oblongs where windows once stood, covered now with frayed white sheets. There are long red benches and tangled blue chairs, a service counter and beyond that the outlines of kitchen equipment and cabinets still clinging to the ceiling.

I kick a path through tumbled chairs and throw the first cabinet door open, to find it is stocked with cans of pineapple slices. In the next are meatballs, dry pasta and cans of stored vegetables. I grin. This must be the ship's larder, enough to feed the thousands in their ark until the floods dispelled and their God showed them the way forward.

I snatch up a can of pineapples, scrabble for an opener and spoon the first ring into my mouth. Heaven, and my hangover melts away. Unfortunately the whispered voices do not.

As it grows dark, and I work through three cans with different contents, their babbling gets louder, as though someone is steadily upping the dial on a speaker. I hold my hands over my ears but it does no good at all.

They start to say my name. They say names I haven't spoken for a decade, as though reflecting my deepest secrets. I catch the name Ven on the air and try to snatch it back before it spreads any wider, but soon they're all saying it, in all their different voices.

Ven.

I've avoided thinking about her for more than ten years, not since I Lagged the weight of her away just to survive, leaving me hollow inside with only these frames and guilt for company. Ven who I lost in the Arctic, who died just like most of us died, in meaningless wars against people who looked just like us, who wanted just what we wanted, like soldiers trapped in filthy black trenches just holding the line. She is the ghost who haunts my life.

Ven. Shit. The voices press her onto me and I punch the table, go back to the cupboard store and come back with a bottle of ancient godship vodka.

Short of an EMR, it's the only way I know.

ME

VEN

I open the book and read to the chord.

Three years in to my time as a Soul Jacker in the Arctic War, I met Ven. She was officer class and a cold cold bitch. Everybody hated her. Heclan my assistant in the jacks said, "I heard she eats ice and shits out Freon."

I remembered it because later on when I told it to Ven in bed, she said, "I'll have him demoted two classes," which was funny in itself, then she said, "Freon is a gas, the idiot, it'd have to be frozen CO_2," which was funnier still. "You can't eat a gas."

Ven had some kind of social disability, perhaps one of the mild Autisms gene-coded to make her more palatable for service on a subglacic.

Accordingly, she was a genius of administration and management, able to quantify the output of a threat-matrix faster than any unmodified conscript. Because of her, our subglacic evaded any number of dry-ice bombs left to percolate in the icepack, as well as several mindbombs dropped via depth charge from the Schooner-class warships overhead, until the last one took us all, which was my fault.

She and I were unlikely to ever cross paths as anything more than resident Soul Jacker liaising with the captain, and then only after a successful raid on an enemy outpost or drilling rig, when the prisoners would be shuffled into the thumping pulse of my Electro-Magnetic Resonance machine and I would jack them for secrets.

We met because of Heclan, and CSF vodka, and one of the days I nearly died.

Heclan was my assistant and he made vodka fermented from artificial Cerebro-Spinal Fluid, in a complex filtration system he wangled together by buying parts from the marine twins Tigrates and Ferrily, who stole them from the outposts we raided.

Before every raid Heclan would ruffle back his thick mop of brown hair and draw up an illicit brewer's shopping list filled with laboratory retorts, round-bottomed flasks, tiptration condensers, hose-tubing and reflux drums, then deliver it to the twins, who would try to hunt those items down and claim them as spoils of the War.

CSF vodka tasted like piss with vinegar, but we toasted our own health with it, toasted the bounties tallying up in our accounts onshore, toasted the amounts of icepack we'd blown apart and the other idiots we'd blasted to make a few yards distance, then drank ourselves paralytic.

I met Ven when Heclan screwed up by labeling a fermented bag of CSF in place of an unfermented one, then inadvertently loaded it into the coolant channels for my next jack.

Both the target and I were three thousand sheets to the wind and piss-drunk beyond all conception within a matter of seconds. Our brains were bathed in raw alcohol to a level pretty much unheard of in history, so much that it flooded the three-layered brick shell of my sublavic ship to the tip of the conning tower, screwing me up beyond all recognition.

Chaos was inescapable after that, having breached the blood-brain barrier. Even unconsciousness could not get it out. After a few moments of utter chaos as my mind ballooned and shrank, I died, as did the target.

Naturally Ven was called. One glance at the readings told her what had happened, and she tossed both me and the target into artificial wombs to keep our hearts going and replace our corrupt CSF, then with a hammer and surgical chisel cracked open our heads one after the other like eggshells, to let the poison out.

Then she jacked into me. I can't quite imagine what that phantasmagoric freakscape must have been like, or quite why she

Soul Jacker

decided to do it, but probably it had something to do with the threat matrix and needing whatever insights I'd already jacked from the target's Soul.

She managed to tap my Solid Core for the seven tones of my Soul which she chimed throughout my brain. That kept my mental architecture alive long enough for the womb to bring me back around.

I was drunk for days afterward. There was no one left to jack the target, and he died despite the artificial womb. Heclan explained the accident away on a batch of faulty CSF, which was just believable enough as it had happened other times too, and in private offered to quit the War and pay me all his onshore bounties as restitution.

I told him I'd kill him if he ever did it again. He nodded his brown bob solemnly and we toasted the pact with a fresh batch of foul liquor. They were different times, in the thick of the War. Death was always a bad ice floe away.

Then Ven came.

I thought it must be for the information I'd gleaned, but it turned out to be the opposite. She was there about information she'd gleaned in me, and how it had disturbed her. She was not a Jacker in any more than certification, as all captains were then required to be, and she wasn't used to the influx of another person's mind.

She suggested we have sex, and I consented.

Lying in each others' arms afterward, after the rhythmic pulsations were done and all our hollering was finished, she wept, which perhaps she hadn't done ever in her life. It was my gift to her, perhaps, my broken Soul holding up a mirror to hers.

The sex became regular. I came to see the beauty in her, despite her fierce and analytical front. She was never soft in front of me, never self-piteous, but always raw. She lit up my emotions like a blowtorch, kept me guessing at every step. I never knew if she would kick like a wild horse or wrap me up in hot passion like a choking squid. She was as irrepressible as a force of nature.

Our affair was wild, heady and it changed us both. While she never grew soft, she softened. Humor crept into her dealings with the crew, while a little of her fierce intellect infected me. Our mutual

105

passion endured while a solid core of loyalty, faith and even love crept up between us.

"You're the ice king now," Heclan said. "Do you shit Freon too?"

"It should be frozen CO_2," I corrected him.

Tigrates and Ferrily thought it was great, and constantly teased me about what she'd do to me once we broke up. Perhaps I'd be left as a target after the next raid, or abandoned floating on a tiny raft of pack ice, drifting away across the Arctic.

We didn't break up. After six months we began to talk about a future away from the ice, making a home and having dozens of children and to hell with the population controls, behind a tsunami wall on one of the high latitude mountains of Calico.

"You bear one, then I'll bear one, then one for the artificial womb," she said, pointing between us. Even then it was a possibility for a man to bear a child.

"We'll name them after our missions," she said.

"What are our mission names?" I asked, because I never knew, I was always too deep down in the ship and drunk to care.

She reeled off the lists from memory, each named after a population center closest to the infraction zone:

Yakut Even

Kutchin Hare

Yukagahir

Naskapi

Iquliat

Chukchi Koryak

Athabascan

Places where ancient Inuit peoples once lived, dark-skinned snow-dwellers that we turfed out like we turfed out everyone, as the habitable belt of our world shifted north and the oceans rose.

We talked about morality and death, about the War and the point of it all. I explained how it always seemed that all our efforts merely flexed at the territory lines, pushing them out and pulling them in like the tide.

"We never gain," I said. "Marines just die and it's pointless."

"Maybe death is the point," Ven answered. "There are too many people on this planet."

She knew all the details of deaths and square acreage, had figures at the ready, and I think they helped convince her that the War was a good thing. Besides, if we didn't fight then one of the other coalitions would win, and that would lead to an unacceptable monopoly of power and wealth. In that sense, we weren't fighting for victory, but for a stabilized détente amongst a reduced number of competitors.

I came to understand that from her, as she came to understand from me that détente was a hard proposition to ask people to die for. We both changed, molding to fit in each other's worlds, to both of our benefits. The softness I nurtured in her made her a better, more empathetic captain. The cool outlook she brought to me made me a better, more analytical jacker.

In the end, I think it was my softness that led her to get us all killed, and her hardness that kept me alive while everyone else died.

The choice was to bomb a civilian ship skirting the old Alaskan perimeter. Every sign it gave showed its age and the presence of refugees aboard. It was not even over the boundary line, merely on the edge.

The old Ven would have sunk it without a second thought, and scavenged amongst its survivors for some targets to jack for intel. The new Ven hesitated and gave the ship time to turn around, perhaps thinking of the children we had promised each other.

It was enough.

They dropped a mindbomb on us, an Electro-Magnetic Pulse for the nervous system. They were banned weapons even then, similar in scope to the biological weapons of the past that killed everything organic but left the enemy's infrastructure in place, ripe for annexation.

The mindbomb disrupted electrical and magnetic fields at a level so minute it would not cause a subglacic's engines or systems to falter. Perhaps a few digital clocks in the crew bedrooms would overload and fuse. Along with them, every bit of human matter controlled by electrical impulse was overloaded at once.

Grand mal seizures killed every member of the crew. Their brains stopped functioning, their hearts stopped pumping, their limbs stopped holding them up and their breath halted as they were simply switched off.

That is how Ven and all my friends died.

I alone survived, caught in the middle of an EMR cycle. Along with my jack target, I was protected by the EMR's electromagnetic field, which thumped on as Heclan died at the controls, as Tigrates and Ferrily died, as everyone died.

I was left trapped, with no one to switch off the machine and let me out, but thanks to Ven's analytical influence I didn't panic. I hid from the Lag within my target's mind, tossing what memories of hers I could to buy time, until there were none left. Then I fled back to my own Molten Core, and fed the Lag all the non-essential things I could afford to lose, the weight and frames both in the end, until I had to make real choices about what I most needed to keep.

I held onto the memory of Ven and my friends, but perhaps I had other friends that I gave up. I will never know, because now they're gone. I gave up all the fringe parts of my childhood, keeping in place only the worst of it and the best of it, to prevent permanent change to my Soul. I gave up my knowledge of everything; how to walk and breath and run and talk. I fed off pieces of myself to the Lag like a cannibal dressing his own limbs for dinner, all the while calling through the EMR links for Heclan to let me out.

The enemy let me out two days later.

Marines switched off the EMR and finally I surfaced, to their disbelief. No one had lived that long in the middle of a Soul jack. They kept me alive in a womb as a scientific miracle, perhaps sustained due to the odd architecture of my seven-toned mind.

They studied me and jacked me, hunting for the reason I had survived for so long. Even after the War came to its anticlimactic end, researchers continued to come to my recovery pod, begging me to make a run on the Solid Core and open the door to the hidden knowledge within. If anyone could do it, they felt, it would be me.

But I had no interest in that. I had nothing left, having cored myself of who I was, leaving only a skeleton for ragged clumps of meat to hang upon. I had a heart filled with Ven, and some organs that lived for Heclan, Ferrily and Tigrates, and that was all.

But they were all dead.

I was a freak, worse than the jackers who'd Lagged themselves to death in the Solid Core, because I had come back, and was massively diminished. Once I finally learned how to speak and to move again I fled and kept running until I hit the neon Skulks of proto-Calico, where I drank and whored my onshore bounties away in stupor and flesh until the tsunami wave was forecast to come, promising to bring its final, lasting erasure.

I stop reading, and a long silence fills the aftermath. There are tears in Ray's eyes. He reaches out to Far and takes the boy in his arms. I look to Doe, blurry through the tears in my own eyes.

I remember Ritry Goligh, now. I wrap my arms around Doe, working them underneath the shoulder-cannon and accelerator. Perhaps she even cries too. I remember who Ven is, and what she means. I feel again the surging righteousness of this mission we are on, to take back all these things that have been stolen from us.

Someone is hurting Ritry Goligh, and I know I will do anything to save him. We are his chord, and we owe our lives to him.

I pull back and see the same revelation in Doe's eyes. These are weapons we can use.

thump thump

thump thump

The pulse grows louder. The hatch cover bangs against Ray's broad back. We are off So's route in my HUD, but there's nothing else to do.

"For Ritry Goligh," Doe says, and fires her cannon into the opposite wall, which rips like wet wool through to the tunnel beyond.

RITRY GOLIGH

10. BONDS

I can't go back.

I rouse with this thought foremost in my mind, lying with one arm splayed off the bed in a bright room. It is a thought whole and complete, without fear or regret. It is a new foundation to build upon.

I open my eyes to sunlight. The glare blinds me and I roll to my feet, pawing for the window blind, but this is not my apartment on Skulk 47 and I come up against glass. The surface is hot and I crack open my eyes. Inch by inch, a glorious view is unveiled.

The godship fleet lies spread below me in ruin, burnished to a startling copper glow by the dawn sun, like a metal mountain range. Every contour of broken hull seems starkly alive, sparkling in the orange morning light. Hints of green jump out from the rusted ship graveyard, where windblown grass and small trees have nestled into culverts in the battered metal. Pink Arctic cherry blossoms spray across the red and white hulls like snowfall.

I stand transfixed. My old view over blue tarps and homeless people on Skulk 47 seems so far away, as though the realm of an entirely different person. Bathed in this glow I remember the night before; staggering through the corridors of this twice-abandoned cathedral ship, cursing every god I could think of between swigs of vodka, for Ven and Heclan, for Tigrates and Ferrily and most of all for myself.

Then I dreamed, and they were all with me. We ran through the ruined godships like children, skating over the waves on jetskis, laughing and loving with all my old friends and lovers together again.

Then I wake to this. It feels like bliss.

"You begin to see," comes a voice from behind.

I know that this is Mr. Ruin. I even know what he will say; the intent building in the air like the rising smell of dust before a storm.

I turn to face him. He stands at the door dressed in dapper gray; a smart gray waistcoat with black toggle buttons, a crisp white shirt open at the throat, gray sharply pressed suit trousers above black dress shoes. On his chin is a grizzled peppery stubble. His nose is aquiline and lean, his tan cheeks bright, his dark hair buzzed close to the scalp. The lines on his face mark him to be somewhere about forty, though he must be far older, if what he said about watching my artificial womb is true. His gray eyes burn with the reflected dawn and his teeth shine a polished ceramic white.

Mr. Ruin. Everything about him exudes a genteel Calico class. I wonder if I should cut his throat or thank him.

"You," I say.

He smiles, dashes off the slightest of bows and in that brief moment I might have had him, if I'd wanted, might have brained him with an elbow or knee, but something holds me back.

"Me," he says.

We study each other, and the orange glow of dawn fades through the window, back to a normal Arctic gray. The room goes dull.

"You set me up," I say, letting it all roll out. "You killed the Don's son, you sent Mei-An to hook me in then you waited at the shark arena. You laid out a suit for me and I put it on."

He regards me coolly, as though waiting politely for me to go on. I do.

"You've made it so I can't go back. No doubt Don Zachary's already repossessed the jack-site and my apartment, and killed Carrolla if he didn't get out. He'll have all the Skulks hunting me down. You've snipped off my old life like some errant hair." He seems particularly pleased with this metaphor. "What I want to know is why? What could it possibly be for?"

Even as I'm speaking I work my peripheral vision around the room scanning for a weapon, but there's nothing I can use. The room is plain and functional, probably just as it had once been in its godship days.

Ruin clears his throat politely. "I believe in potential, Ritry. I have watched and guided you all your life, so it should come as no surprise to hear that your potential is unique. You are capable of far greater power on the bonds than I, or indeed even the King himself. Would such a comparison offend you?"

I frown. King? Bonds? "What the fuck are you talking about?"

His smile broadens. "Coarseness is certainly a part of your charm, though it too is merely a shield, keeping you from the reality you so cravenly seek. Ritry, do not be a child. You well understand what I am saying, and we are both fucking adults here, are we not?"

I grunt. It might be galling to have this psychopath call me a child, if he weren't such a child himself in all his parlor tricks and games. "Stop blathering then. Stop feeding me a line of bullshit. If you care about potential, what about that poor sad case in the Napoleon suit? What kind of fetish is that, by the way? And what about his potential?" I click my fingers. "Cut off at the balls."

Mr. Ruin allows a rich laugh. "Colorful. But what potential did he have, Ritry? The unconsidered life is not worth living, have you heard that expression? His life was deeply unconsidered. He was an animal following a base line of programming written from his birth, and to extinguish him from the bond-lines was no more consequential than the slaughter of a pig for its meat. Another pig will simply rise to take his place."

"That is just weird," I say. "I hope you didn't take a bite out of him."

He laughs again. "So angry. Ritry, dead flesh is of no consequence to me. The true vitality comes from the living, and the trails they leave behind. But to take your deeper, unintended point, in that sense did I take a bite from him? Only in the most ephemeral sense, and in no way that would impact him beyond death. It wasn't very nourishing or flavorful, but then I take my meals when the opportunity presents."

A long moment passes in which I say nothing, just look at him. He seems content to merely look back at me. Is he talking about eating people or not? He doesn't have a weapon. Perhaps I could rush him, take him down and have an end to it, but I just don't know enough.

"You're mad," I say instead.

"To you, I know I seem it. But then why are you here? Are you mad too? Everything you have said so far, you knew before you came. You could have taken the old man's speedboat in any direction, to any city. You could have crossed the wall into Calico yourself, as you advised your good friend. A new life would await you on the other side, but instead you came here. What does that say about you, Ritry?"

That is a galling question, because I have no good answer. A glib answer, that this seemed safer, more isolated, will not suffice. His gaze only pisses me off more, so I draw it away. His folder lies on the floor by my feet, and I pick it up. "I felt like taking a vacation. This is some kind of travel guide?"

"An avoidance tactic? Very well. It is an education. Tell me, Ritry, how did you dream last night?"

An involuntary shudder rushes through me. Ruin notices and smiles. "I could feel your dreams from here. They were good, the best you've had in years, were they not? That was the balm of forgiveness, of a clean break. That is my gift to you. It remains to be seen how you will invest the capital."

I ignore him and instead flick through the folder, to the first page now buried somewhere in the middle. It is stained with Carrolla's blood, crumpled and spattered. I scan the page to the bottom and read it aloud.

"'There is power here, Ritry, if you dare to take it.' What's that about?"

Ruin smiles wide, showing those crazy white shark teeth. "Why ask when you already suspect? Here, let me ease you in." He taps his cane smartly on the deck, and I blink, tracking it. Did he have a cane before? "Do you know the story of Napoleon, Ritry, the would-be Emperor of a nation called France? It may shock you to learn I was there with him for it all; through his days as Emperor, through his banishment on Elba, through his resurgence and back to exile again. You know this faintly, I believe, from a memory injected in your War days. But then I am quite old. To the point, however, you will not know of his second resurgence; the time he swept the Gaullic coast clean of pretenders and when the blood of his rivals ran in the ornate halls of Versailles. You will not know it, because I took it all."

He snatches at the air with one gray-gloved hand. "I took the whole memory of it; 'Lagged', you would say, from his 'Soul' and from all the 'Souls' that might know it, and it was delicious. It made me strong, because Ritry, I am a predator." His teeth gleam menacingly. At that moment a rain cloud passes over the sun and the room grows cold. "I am a predator and so are you. We exist to hunt, and shorn of the hunt we are nothing. I suspected it in you from the start, and so I have watched you throughout. Why else are you so pathetic? No, don't deny it, you are. It is because you have curtailed yourself, locked yourself within a feeble, diminished life; a lion living off grass and leaves. It sickens me because it is unspeakably selfish. You are squandering such immense potential. I hope to unleash that potential and reshape the world, through turning the bonds on their head."

I have to will myself not to take a step back. What began as faintly amusing if bizarre is now repellently charismatic. The madness seems to burn up off him in waves, glowing through his cheeks.

"Napoleon was hundreds of years ago," I say, "you're no more than fifty."

Ruin laughs again, and the density of the madness radiating off him lessens. "Quite right. I am yet young, and in my prime! But answer me this, and be honest with yourself if not with me. You feel something here and it has fuelled you, has it not? You feel invigorated, flush with new strength. Why, your customary hangover has even failed to materialize. Wonders, praise the Lord! But heed this, Ritry. Dreams do not come from nothing. They are memories on the eternal bonds, trapped as though in amber, and the old power of this place," he stretches his arms out to encompass the godship, "has entered you, though you did not seek it. Seek it directly and the flow will be so much stronger. There is power in these bonds, Ritry, in the memories and traces through space we humans leave behind. There is power in breaking the bonds of life and memory just as there is in breaking the bonds of an atom. To that end, you have begun down your trail of crumbs." He points at the folder. "Follow the trail or do not, but do not try to bullshit me. The paths lie before you. Can you truly turn away now?"

I drop the folder on the bed. "You're talking about harvesting the power of the Solid Core."

Ruin clicks his fingers. "Precisely. It is a resource just as the hydrates under the Arctic pack were, worthy of fighting over. And out here, what is the cost? Every Soul who left their pattern in this place is long gone or dead. To swallow the marrow of their past is no different from gathering corn grown with the sun."

"Or slaughtering a pig."

"Ha! Indeed. Perhaps you will come to see that the two are not so very different. Did you grieve for your lost lover, Ven, when the mindbomb dropped upon your subglacic, or were you too busy scrabbling to survive? Life is a war, Ritry, and right now you are its biggest loser. But is that all you are, casualty of a specific kind of surrender? Are you the lion who will not bloody his claws or fangs for the pain it will cause his prey? So the lion pines and dies, and what does he honor any living thing that he will not do as his nature dictates, to the best of his ability? Whom do you honor, Ritry, to deny your own potential? Napoleon fought until the last and I honor him for it. He has become a part of everything I do, and in this I preserve him. Can any man hope for better?"

I point at the folder. "So this is training. To bloody my claws."

Mr. Ruin shrugs. "You will decide that. I will be watching. And remember, I too am a lion, though one far more powerful than you, and I have slaughtered other lions before. Should you disappoint? I need say no more, as you have seen my work in the McAvery's arena. Should you pursue your own potential on the bonds, however, and within the depths of the Solid Core? We will be Kings of this world together, Ritry. All others will tremble at our feet."

He lets that choice hang for a moment. He talks pretty, but it boils down to a basic decision.

"I do what you say or I die," I say, putting it as bluntly as I can.

He smiles. "I would never be so coarse. But yes, in essence. Yet it's not much of a life to lose, is it? Skulking on the floating slums, hiding your light under a bushel. It would more be putting you out of your misery." His smile widens and his teeth catch the gray light. "Though the misery would not be over swiftly, I promise you that. I would dine well on your potential for years. Think about that, and farewell for now, Ritry Goligh. May your training be everything you wish for."

He turns and strides from the room. I stand frozen for a moment as though I have been Lagged. His footsteps clang away, until abruptly they stop. I follow him out and peering up and down the habitation corridor, but of course there is no sign of him. Was he ever here? I wonder if I might be able to track his movements through the 'eternal bonds', if such things truly exist.

I shudder to consider it. Did Mr. Ruin just command me to murder people and eat their Souls? I'm not so sure. He is undoubtedly mad, or mad from the viewpoint of the world I have always known, but perhaps that too is a kind of sane; just one that I have never considered before.

Hmm.

The strange thing is, I'm not alarmed. The effect of the dream is still with me, and the dawn has buoyed me up. In fact I feel a ravenous hunger, but not for more canned goods. I have a taste for something else now, something far more powerful, and I cannot see the harm. The people here are gone and cannot be hurt any further.

I start back through the dead cathedral ship with the memories of a thousand lost Souls rubbing up against my mind, as if the ship itself is a Molten Core and I am the Lag.

11. YLEP

I have lost everything, but I feel better than I have in years. Standing at the highest point of the godship complex, atop a makeshift section of metal decking riveted to the Ylep's keel, I feel alive.

The Arctic Ocean swirls in the Arctic Basin, spinning down the drain we dug with all our depth charge explosions, and I feel good. The sky is gray, the sea is gray, and I can never go back to the Skulks again. I have lost Carrolla, who was the closest thing I had to a friend, I have lost the home and habits that saved me when the tsunami never came, and I feel like a weight has been lifted off.

It feels like forgiveness for all my many crimes.

Tears roll down my cheeks as I breathe in the fresh rain and salt air. There used to be ice in all these places. We are not only parasites come to consume the decay left behind, we are predators too, come to take what is ours. I am a predator, and always have been.

The cathedral ship lifts me, and I can feel the waves of memory Mr. Ruin spoke of rising like an EMR tide. Probably I can ride them, if I try.

I leaf through the folder he left behind, skimming the story of the godships; cruiseliners repurposed into arks, each carrying some five thousand of the faithful along with thousands of plants and animals. Cathedral ships, was the name they used. I've seen footage of them in their prime; vast city-states that drifted serenely on the rising waters like mini-Calicos, each geared with the best flood defenses and buoyancy aids money could buy.

They roamed the empty middle oceans far from any land, on the theory that they were unsinkable and too heavy to carry far enough to dash upon the rocks of the nearest landmass.

Back then, when the wall around Calico was half its current height, the godships seemed the safest place in the world. Their sermons became legendary, broadcast around the narrowing, shrinking coastal cities of the world. They were a light that people looked to, the hope to restart creation if the long-predicted global tsunamis finally came about. We had torn up the sky and torn up the sea, and their god's wrath was coming to strike us all down.

Then it came, and it struck the cathedral ships first. They were at their yearly convocation near the pole when the great Arctic ridge burst wide open. The global tsunami hit and kept hitting, as the planet's crust vented massive internal pressures. Wave after wave lofted their ships and shifted them inexorably toward coastal barriers.

The chaos lasted for days and they broadcast throughout, confident in their faith. But the waves kept on coming, and coming, and as half the world perished in flooding, so every last godship in the world was swept thousands of miles to break on distant mountain slopes.

There was no escape for them, and no survivors. Their god's flood, which they thought would save them and scour the world, only served to scour the world of them and their god.

I can feel their Souls now, rising beneath me in this graveyard of thousands. I feel not only their growing terror as the last days drove them to their death, but everything else as well: the ties of love and faith between lovers and families and friends, all the good times and bad built upon each other like layers of cells in a brain. They stretch out forward and backward, massed around this spot where their threads in the bond-weave of consciousness were abruptly pinched off.

They make me strong. Both the good and the bad lift me up, like radioactive isotopes harnessed for enormous power. I only need to plunge into this weave like I would plunge into a Soul jack, and squeeze.

I do it. I reach out like I'm reaching out within an EMR, feeling for the flows in the godship wreckage and synchronizing my thought patterns with theirs; like a jack but with no Molten Core or Lag, only a great field grown ripe with the past.

I sink in my teeth.

Wellbeing floods through me. Old bonds rupture and release a power I've never felt before, rushing like a drug. I have never felt so strong, so confident, so self-assured. The lives of these people billow like wind in my sail, saying this is my place and this is my world, and I cannot be stopped. I not only feel smarter and more competent than ever before, but I become those things. I become a better version of myself, buoyed by a sense of belonging and ownership I've never felt before, in this world that never wanted me. I am more real now than I ever was.

Seagulls flock in the air above and I feel their tiny Souls like hot dots on a sonar screen, each a tiny molten lake swathed around a pellet-like Solid Core. I reach out further to the oceans; there are orca hunting a school of fish, and I feel their Souls too. Hotter than the birds, concealing deep and heavy Cores, they respond to my touch.

I tell the orca to swim to the surface. I command the birds to fly to meet them. In instant after glorious instant they come beak to beak, these inhabitants of such different worlds, and I luxuriate in the power. Now I see that I never needed an EMR to do this. I just needed the will.

I stride along the Ylep's keel top feeling like I could spread my own wings and fly. From the high tip of the ship's broken middle a pair of wires shoots away to anchor in another wreck, and I walk out atop them without a second thought, because I know instinctively that this power is not limited other Souls.

This power can transform my own. With it I feel the wind and the sway of the cables like an extension of my body. My Soul expands to encompass these things, and I learn to walk the tightrope as if it is level ground. Everything I need is here; I breathe the world and it buoys me up, as if this is the most natural thing there is.

The Ylep fades behind me and I sway above a lethal fall to the frothy rocks below, more alive than ever. Every sway in the wire is known to me already, as though we are one, bringing the simple and certain knowledge that I will never fall. My feet will not slip because I am their master. I am master of all of this through the bonds left behind.

Halfway along I begin to run, because I can. The wire jolts and bounces and I jolt and bounce along with it, in perfect harmony.

At the bottom I leap off onto a landing gantry amongst the rocks. The wreck here offers a section of forecastle split off from its hull like a boulder sheared along a fault line. I climb into it with ease, avoiding broken glass and toothy snarls of metal, onto a level corridor which many thousands of people walked before me. I can feel all their bonds branching out like a web.

I enter the cathedral ship's inner temple through a large archway, twisted to the side like a dislocated shoulder. Before me stretches a vast and towering space filled with hundreds of long wooden pews, lined up before an altar marked with icons from all the world's major religions.

The weight of belief here drops me to my knees and forces tears from my eyes. Light streams in through high broken windows, painting the central aisle a vivid red and turning the pews a welcoming mahogany. It is beautiful, holy, and the mass of intersecting bonds is beyond overwhelming. It is rapture.

When I come back to myself the bars of light have shifted, and I feel full up to the brim. Everything I'd hunted for in the days after Ven and the war; scrounging around the Skulks hunting for a reason to be alive, all the while fighting for scraps in brothels and bar-fights, fighting against others just to get a taste; all of that is here in abundance. I can feel every Soul that passed this way and left their trace as an individual note in this grand symphony of memory. They are imprinted in me now too.

And I don't hurt a single living Soul to do it, unlike Mr. Ruin, no more than a gliding gull hurts the wind. They didn't know what they left behind in life and none of them will miss it in death. I could live here for a thousand years and never need anything else.

But I can't stay. Being here has changed me, and Mr. Ruin was right about what he promised, because now I've found something to want.

More.

12. SKULK 47

Back at the Ylep as the sun sets, I siphon gas from the jet-skis into Don Zachary's speedboat. The sky grows dark but I have never felt less tired.

Easing the boat through the sharp reefs is so easy that I could do it with my eyes closed, sensing the outline of rocks beneath the water. Full dark falls as I pull onto open ocean and accelerate over the low breakers. Wind streams through my hair and a sky full of stars sparks to life above. The bonds of the godship fleet snap away from me one by one, but the charge they injected remains.

I stand up before the wheel and shout into the sky. Everything is open and everything is to play for now. Mr. Ruin's folder of locations is warm at my chest, and I wonder if I really am the predator he named me to be. Could I ever break living bonds and serve as a kind of living, vampiric Lag growing strong off their loss?

How would that feel, if I did?

I cannot imagine it. In all my years as a Soul Jacker I have built connections. Even when I jacked marines' minds to steal information in the War, I never destroyed what I found, merely brought it to the surface. I fought the Lag and staved it off where I could, always trying to build.

What strange power there must be in destruction. I tear into the night following the trails hanging in the air around me and hungry for more.

Docking at Skulk 47, everything feels different. The tawdry neon alley I walked every day for ten years now reads as a tangled knot of intersecting traces; hot and cold with passion, anger, the stinging efflorescence of sex and the bile of violence and addiction with countless sub notes of ownership, pain, love, loss, loneliness and hunger.

The godships have opened my eyes. All these threads now seem distinct and familiar and I pick through them in my mind. Here are my old traces; a solitary line woven back and forth ten thousand times along the same route. Here is a red-haired girl from the brothel, here is Carrolla my assistant, here is Don Zachary's blazing line, and his son's and Mei-An's all overlapping like a massed tangle of bright wool.

The alley burns like a furnace. I could thrive off these, if only they'd stay as clear as they are right now, though I know they won't. Already I can see the bonds begin to fade, and without the immense, clarion faith of the godships to boost me along I soon won't be able to pick them apart at all.

I can't let that happen now. I can't choose to be blind after seeing such light.

I dock the speedboat and drag a molding, half-disintegrated green canvas sheet out of the seafoam to cover it as best I can, then I start up the alley.

My jack-site has been repossessed already. The door is fenced off and the trail of Don Zachary goes in and out like a fresh trail of slug slime. There'll be nothing left for me inside, so instead I follow the Don's thread.

It leads me down the alley, through the pimps and whores and masseuse boys and girls and touts, still out parading their wares at this early hour of the morning. They stare at me like I'm a dead man waking, when in truth I am Napoleon come for his second resurgence, ready to bring the world to its knees.

I smile at them. I'm sure they have heard what happened to Carrolla. They know Don Zachary is looking for me, and here I come by with a smile. I am radioactive and they shrink away.

The Don's line follows mine and Mei-An's back through the Skulk slums and past the sagging pond in the blue tarp park. In the darkness I spy the homeless marine, and he looks back at me with eyes that burn with a hundred dead in the Arctic depths. I can feel his trace arcing north to the bloody ice of the War, where his mind dwells even now.

He nods at me and I nod at him, brothers in this.

The Don's thread leads me up the stairs to my apartment. It is a ransacked wreck. The mattress has been torn into foamy pieces, my breakfast chair and tables have been smashed and the walls have been ripped back to wooden scaffold. The alarm clock no longer sheds red light, its white shell fractured with its innards crunching underfoot. My clothes lie tossed around like sun-dried kelp, my seaweed bread has had chunks bitten out of it and my toaster is dented.

It looks like one of the rooms in the godships, with all the belongings left behind as though the owner expected one day to come back. I see my own trace knotted brightly on the air in hot zones of thought and activity; my track backward through the last ten hopeless years.

Now it's a ruin.

Don Zachary has done this to me. I reach out along his thread on the bonds like I'm jacking a Molten Core, hunting him down until I sense him ten Skulks over; hidden in the depths of his bunker, surrounded by his marines and his harem and his children both adult and infant, asleep.

He dreams of revenge.

So do I. I stride out of my old apartment like a butterfly pupating from its cocoon, hard upon the trail of the Don.

13. DON ZACHARY

Don Zachary owns an entire Skulk. In truth he owns them all, and I can see that ownership glowing in the air like colorful tracer rounds; his path linking him to every floating barge in proto-Calico.

I slow the speedboat engine as I draw near to the Skulk's central dock. There are marines there with Kaos rifles held at the ready, dressed in the black regalia of Hawks; mercenaries who fought in all theaters of the War, for all coalitions.

Don Zachary's path shoots through their chests too. It shoots through mine, and leads to a tightly-woven nest at the heart of the Skulk where the Don is rumored to have built himself a tsunami-proof bunker.

The dock is circled by a tall plate metal wall, and there are Hawks up there manning howitzers. I sense them rouse as my speedboat comes into range of their floodlights.

"Stop there," a voice calls out, and they point their weapons my way. Bullets rake the dark water before me as a warning, but I do not stop. Instead I reach out and pluck at the threads between me and these marines even as they form. I follow them back through the air like I would in the EMR, jacking straight into their Molten Cores where the threads between us plug in neatly: their eyes, their ears, all the means they use to sense the world.

I unplug them.

It is so easy, like smoothing a surface-level engram in the jackroom, with Carrolla watching over from above and the EMR machine shaping the electromagnetic soup around me, except I don't need an EMR machine anymore. I am a fission reactor burning hot, able to Lag bonds with my mind alone, and each one serves to drive on the chain reaction. Even as I pull their switches and work the Lag,

I remember Mr. Ruin doing the same thing in the shark arena; dropping Zachary's thugs with a thought.

I have that same power now. It is intoxicating; a better high than the godships. The jolt of power from each one spooling free is substantial. They heighten my senses and increase my reach, recharging the slow dwindle of the godships' vigor. I have never Lagged a waking soul before, and never felt anything like this.

It feels indescribably good.

I pluck at their Souls like a virtuoso banjo-ist, keeping my presence in their minds as nothing more disturbing or important than the ache in their legs from standing duty all night. Though they see me, I prevent them from really seeing me. I'm like a ghost walking before them in plain sight.

They do not fire as I pull up and rope in. I could flex my muscles and Lag them all into puddles on the dock, if I wanted. I control what they see and how they feel about what they see.

"Sir, you can't park that here," one of them says, his eyes lukewarm and calm as a gentled shark. He can barely see me.

"It's the Don's boat," I say, and let this slip through for them all. It means they will guard this boat as though it is the Don's until I return.

"But who are you?" the man asks. His dull face is vaguely quizzical. Just following a rote script, barely realizing what he's saying. "Does the Don expect you?"

"Yes," I say, and pull the weight out of the lie before it sees me shredded by howitzer from above. It is so easy now, with every struck bond of fresh-forming memory providing more energy than it takes to break it. Their minds want to recoil against me, are waiting for the weight of a clear observation to tell them to, but I don't give them that chance. "Can you let me through please?"

"We're not supposed to," a man says from above.

I chuckle. "Would you prefer I climb?"

I let the chuckle and the warmth through. They are professionals, cold killers as ruthless as I ever was, as cold as Ven before I softened her a little, but like Ven they will respond to warmth in the complete absence of threat. For them, there is nothing here to fight.

The man before me smiles uneasily. "No, sir, of course not. Well, let's open it up."

I wink. "Just a crack will be enough. I can slip through."

"Of course, sir."

A section of the wall lifts up to my left. I nod briskly and make for it.

"Carry on," I say, and they do, all interaction between us Lagged and forgotten.

Inside the wall lies a weakly lit passage that smells of urine and seaweed-tobacco ash. The Don's line here is hot and recent. A few industrial drying lamps pour out hot orange light. A camera array above records my face, reporting it to Hawks ahead who I feel begin to react, but this is no concern. I reach out and quiet them from a distance.

Through the passageway I emerge into a wide courtyard spread with white marble chips, where a dozen ancient cars are parked. I walk amongst them, these collectibles scoured from a forgotten era and useless on the Skulks, trailing my fingers over their sleek, gloss-metal lines.

BMW

ROLLS ROYCE

PORSCHE

LAMBOURGHINI

The gravel crunches underfoot, and I notice the absence of any give in the flotation devices. Perhaps there are none, and this part of the Skulk is actually rooted deep down in the seabed. Maybe this whole facility is Zachary's unsinkable bunker.

I stalk on, following his trail and stilling every thread of memory that leaps out from my body before it can dart back through the eyes of the person that sees me, preventing them from shooting me on sight. At a gateway I talk through an intercom while soothing the Hawk who monitors it, persuading her to open for me, and she does.

The bunker is a vast maze, but Don Zachary guides me. I walk down long halls filled with the bright lights and syrupy smell of narcotic hydroponics, where attendants work busily at their product like my old friend Heclan on his CSF still.

I pass down a long corridor of dormitories, sensing more ex-Hawks in the rooms either side, off their shift, some sleeping. They are all thugs drawn from the Skulks, though some of them have families too. I feel the hot tang of Don Zachary's children mixed in amongst them, adult and infant both. The Don's thread is everywhere now, like a suffocating purple web.

I ride an elevator down and emerge in the Don's private mansion. A grand hall extends away from me, and everywhere I look there's a wealth of sheer salvaged silk and vat-grown mahogany, the fur of extinct creatures used for curtaining and rugs, ancient bones used to hold up a coffee table. Through four grand halls I proceed, each more opulent than the last. The solid cement ceiling overhead has been disguised with Romanesque flourishes and elaborate skirting, but I can feel the weight of it bearing down. All of this is tsunami-proof; nothing less for the Don.

I find him in a four-poster bed in a large circular room. It is dark but I find my way by following his hot trail. There are women sleeping in alcoves all around the room, each a colorful buzz of thoughts raised on a small dais, with spotlights fitted above. This is his private boudoir, strip club and brothel.

I turn on all the lights, go to his side and nudge him awake.

"You wanted to kill me," I say.

He wakes up fast, and with consciousness and recognition comes rage, hot and red. He goes for my throat, goes for an alarm button by his bed, thinks of the gun beneath his pillow, but I Lag the weight of all those intentions away as soon as they arise and he sags back.

We look at each other.

"I am sorry your son died," I say. "It wasn't me though, or Carrolla or Mei-An. I'll deal with the man who did it. You can remember that."

I let some of his anger spike through the fog I've put him in, to afford him his say. What he does say surprises me.

"I want to hire you."

I have to laugh at that; the schemings of his mind. This is how he has become the Don of so many Skulks, not only through barbarism but through intellect.

"You can't afford me," I say, "and you won't even remember I was here."

He looks at me with some kind of understanding. Perhaps he knows something about the Lag too. He saw Mr. Ruin's notes after all, and he sees me here now, unharmed in the heart of his bunker.

"Please don't hurt my children," he says.

That plea hits me like a punch in the face. Upon hearing it, I want to leave. I want to assure him I am not that man, I would not kill them all for some petty vengeance, but I can't afford to say those things now. He is still a killer and a torturer, on a Skulk where we are all killers and torturers of some kind.

So what kind am I?

Outwardly, I nod. I feel sick, but there is still a job to do and only I can do it. I seize hold of his mind and the bonds linking him to me, and I Lag them all. Weight and frame both, I strip his sense of me back to the barest outlines, that there was once a Soul Jacker on Skulk 47.

The unwelcome power of all those broken bonds shoots me through the roof, beyond my control. His hatred is focused and immense, so much more portent than the unformed sensations and relics from the godships.

My mind hovers a mile overhead, hanging in the air above the Skulks and gazing down on the hearts and Souls of every person I have ever touched or known, spotted like hot dots on a map: all the women I've loved and the drinking buddies I've made; the neo-Americans I fought the other night sleeping drunk and scattered around the end-Skulks; my redhead at work even now in my old alley; the marine in the sinking park by my old apartment.

I look wider still, to Calico behind its towering tsunami wall, and see Carrolla. He is alive and healthy, recovering from his nail-branded hands and cursing my name. I see Mei-An in the Reach, distraught at the depths she has fallen to in her parents' eyes, the prodigal daughter starting a new life. There are others here too, scattered throughout this narrow jag of mountain rock off the Arctic Circle; marines I've met and jackers I've worked with, people who helped or hurt me as a child.

I see them all, until the fiery glow of Don Zachary's loss ebbs and I sink back down from the heights of the Lag. He is lying there gazing up at me with rheumy eyes. His women are wakeful in their perches and I Lag the memory of me from them too.

I walk out of his bunker like a wave of darkness and sleep, leaving emptiness and quiet behind. I drop into my speedboat and roar away, both sickened and gladdened by what I have done.

ME

J. FRACTAL

The Lag is waiting for us.

We hurl pieces of our shared past that blow like candlebombs and spray the pulsating walls with waxy Lag-matter.

"Doe take point, Ray and Far middle," I order, and they adopt the positions as though out of old habit on the run. There is so much to say, but also so little, because I know my chord better than I know anything else.

"So," I shout through blood-mic as we run into the darkness off the map, tramping through the thrashing gore of a headless worm. The thumping is everywhere now, coming from all directions. "So, we need a new route!"

Only white static comes through my HUD. We race along at an incline, headed inward, our feet beating a chaotic drumroll. I shout for So again and again but she doesn't answer. We reach another five-way ganglion-intersection and the Lag is already galloping down every tunnel toward us.

"Me?" Doe barks.

"Hold," I call, fashioning another memory-grenade from the taste of Heclan's CSF vodka while I ping So relentlessly. Doe drops to one knee and holds a spark to the cannon fuse, while Ray dual-wields muskets.

thump thump

thump thump

thump thump

They're everywhere around us and I don't know which way to run. So warned against turning off the route and we're already far off.

"We need to move, Me!" Ray shouts, hunkered sideways to shelter Far while firing twin streams of musketballs down two tunnels at once.

"So!" I shout through blood-mic, "So, in the name of La, help us!"

Only static returns. The tunnels billow like thin plastic sheeting as the Lag closes in.

thump thump

thump thump

thump thump

I pull up So's map and spin it, trying to calculate a route through it myself, but I don't have the first clue where to start. Without her flashing red dot I don't even know where we are.

BOOM

Doe fires the cannon and a worm right behind me explodes, its face mangled like the Deathgate, but there's another lolling along behind it only seconds out.

"So!" I scream and throw my grenade; it blows but not fast enough, and the worm's mouth snaps around my leg.

The pain is white-hot and only worsens as it slurps me in like a wet noodle. I am tossed to my back and my other leg is sucked in, and worse than the pain is the sheer horror of this eyeless, faceless, lipless thing swallowing me down.

BOOM

The cannon fires pointblank and a splatter of gore shivs off the thing's milk-white flank, but it slows. Ray falls upon it with his musket bayonets, driving the blades deep then firing them inside, and the creature shudders but still sucks me in up to my chest.

"So!" I cry into blood-mic, "please."

A second Lag hits and snatches Far from Ray's side-holster, gulping him down to the neck in a second. I forge the memory of La like an axe-head in my mind and swing it into the beast's shining intestinal side, cleaving it in two halves that disgorge green and black bile. Ray tears Far out, but the one holding me doesn't slack off at all, and the last thing I see before its jaws close over my HUD is Ray staring back at me with disbelief in his eyes.

"Ven," I manage to gasp through blood-mic, before its acidic digestion short-circuits my suit completely. "Use Ven."

A burst of light follows, then Ray and Doe are hauling me out, dizzy and weak. Behind me is a long pink mass of worm bisected fully along it length, the two halves sagging in a slurry of purplish guts. Similarly split worms twitch down every tunnel, but already more of them are coming.

thump thump

"Far," I ask urgently, wiping thick mucus from my visor. "Is Far OK?"

Blood and viscera coat Doe and Ray and Far in their arms. His suit is synced to Doe and I tune into feel the flow of fluids and shockjacks rushing in. the kid is on the edge.

"We ned to get out of here Me," Doe warns. "I'm out."

I'm out too. I don't know what we just blew, but it was big and there's nothing to replace it. I spin around the ganglion looking down the five swelling tunnels trying to make the call, but there's no way I can guess it. I need help but without So I don't know what to-

"Me," comes the faintest hiss through blood-mic.

Relief floods through me. "So, thank Goligh, we need a route! Nothing matches anymore."

"I know," she says, fainter than ever, so quiet I have to boost the gain on her crackly voice over the thump of more incoming worms. "I'm having trouble focusing. Are you really there, Me?"

"So, please, we need that route!"

"I have one," she says, forlorn. "I understand, Me. I understand, but I feel like there's something important I've forgotten, some part of me."

I know how she feels, but there is no time. "The route, So!"

She slings it to my HUD; another three-dimensional sphere, but it's completely different from the previous one. Where that was a fairly simple series of shells and nodules, this is a labyrinthine mess of knotty intersections and overlapping nodules. It doesn't even look like a sphere any more, though there is still a flashing red dot in the outer layers and a red line worming toward the center.

"What the hell happened?" I pant. "Where's the old map?"

"You went the wrong way," says So. "I had to recalculate."

Directly ahead a new Lag thumps into view, thirty seconds out at best.

"But is this rotational?" I protest, trying to figure out the degree of spin that could build this. "How did it get so complex?"

"Oh," says So, with a little sigh, like I've disappointed her. "You're right. It's not a rotational maze anymore, Me. It's fractal, and it's growing." She says all this in a reedy whisper, like these are her dying confessions. "Every moment you're there it grows denser, replicating in constant variations. There are islands around you where the whole maze is repeated in miniature, and within those mazes there are more mazes where it all repeats again. If you stray off the path into one of those offshoots you'll never escape." She says it like it's nothing, like the words don't mean all of our deaths. "Even if you reach the middle, it'll be the wrong middle, and even if you follow this route perfectly, I still don't know if you'll be able to reach the true Core before that path balloons in complexity too."

It sounds like wind and madness to my ears. "I don't understand," I shout back.

"Listen, Me!" she whispers, suddenly urgent. "What looks like a full-sized path now might only be one eighth of a path, or one sixteenth, or one thousandth! You have to go faster, but as you slough off mass for more speed I don't know if you can gain velocity. The calculations won't tell me if you'll have enough to reach the Core or not."

I don't know what to say to that.

"Don't give me up too, please," So adds at the end. "I've felt the others go. I feel empty. Please don't give me up." She sounds like a lost little girl.

"I won't," I answer, even as I know that I will, if I have to.

thump thump

thump thump

Worms are encircling us. I spin the map and find the next leg in our route the sling it to the others and start off at a run. Far needs to rest and we all need ammunition, but there's none of that to be had here.

"This way," I shout, and together we charge at the Lag, concentrating cannon and musket fire on its eyeless face. I muster the memory of the old War-era nations and wield it like a jousting lance which spikes through the bridge of the Lag's open mouth and pins it to the tunnel roof, allowing us by.

Ahead thers's a nodule and I reach it first; a sludgy purple valve in the wall stopped up with a giant gumball-like clot. "The map leads through here," I say on blood-mic, then heave together with Doe and the ball pops out with a slop.

Inside is another RG-stamped metal room and another giant book. I usher the others in then pull the gumball back into the orifice after us. It jams satisfyingly into its slot with a disgusting sound and a froth of foul-smelling liquid. The thumping of the worms outside quietens.

So's quiet breath is gone from blood-mic. I look at the remnants of my chord. Four of us here, and one lost behind. Far's suit armor has been deeply scored with acid, as has mine. He is shivering and pale-faced.

"We'll be OK," I say, putting my hand on his shoulder. "We're nearly there, I promise. Just a little further." Ray nods at me, pale with blood infused through the suit link. We're all flagging, and every second that we waste now allows the maze to elongate more. Those last few fractions could stretch out forever.

"Another book," Doe says.

"More weapons," Ray says.

I waste no time lifting the cover and starting to read.

K. YOUNG RITRY

I was born from an artificial womb, first child of a new genetic breed to survive, soon to be abandoned by the family who'd bred me to life.

They were the last few holdouts of a godly remnant after the cathedral ships fell, barely eking out a life in a world that had turned against their god in the global tsunami. They had wanted to test their faith with me, a vat-born baby.

Was I as much a living Soul in god's earthly creation as they, or was I less? Was I only flesh and blood without a Soul, or did I too come from their holy spirit?

They soon came to hold in their hearts that I was worse than the former. I was some kind of demonseed; alien in the most alarming way, with my seven-toned Soul. I was false and the way I looked at them, even as I burbled out my first few words, was never right in their eyes.

They put it down to the devil and gave me up.

The second family tried to kill me a hundred different ways. They were as far from religious as the melting ice packs, but equally as mad. They were stone-cold scientists, a family commune of three, two men and a woman who served each other however they saw fit. While they must have put a warm and fuzzy front to the disinterested organization that held me up for adoption until I reached War age, they were anything but warm.

They were Soul Jackers all, and brain surgeons to boot. Their specialty was the infant brain, and its gradual unfolding from a cluster of cells through the curling up of neural tubes like tongues fitting into grooves.

My brain was one of a few thousand like it, and invaluable, but poorly valued. There were other concerns in those days, as whole populations continued to shift away from the planet's fat hot middle, as the Arctic War began in earnest. I was born into war, and I was spoils of war as a child.

They jacked my Molten Core repeatedly. Before I had gained any real sense of self they jacked me together and serially, scratching away samples of thought and pulling them out on long sticky threads, further rupturing and altering my development. They jacked me day after day, sinking deeper to the source of my multiple tones, seeking answers which they sprayed out in experimental papers that no coalition cared enough to explore the ethics of.

These were the early days of Soul Jacking, growing out of slapdash memory-injection and experience massage. It was frontier science, and with everything they discovered from my unusual mind, my adoptive parents helped push the barriers out.

My first memory is of an orange rattle hanging above me. It shakes, and there is a smiling face. Then the rattle is gone. I have forgotten it, because unbeknownst to me the memory has been stolen.

The same rattle appears again, and now it is my second first clear memory, written over the scar where the first memory had been. This makes it deeper, but fundamentally unsound. My simple developing mind, that of a two-year-old, perhaps, mistrusts it.

It too is stolen, then replaced.

It was a simple experiment which they repeated hundreds of times, each one a reset button that sucked up vast quantities of my fledgling concentration. The scar tissue in my mind built up thick like a top-heavy tower, threatening to crush everything around it.

It must have been fascinating to them, to see how the cells of my brain shaped and reshaped themselves in new and alarming ways. My gray matter was not plastic like most children, it was fluid. Where a normal womb-grown infant would hit maximum capacity for regrowth at some point, after which unconsciousness or a total blind spot for orange rattles would develop, my mind did not.

The seven note-architecture allowed my mind to flow continuously, which meant there was no escape, and an almost endless capacity for this game. So my earliest memory is of an orange rattle, again and again, again and again, again and again.

I was helpless. They published papers. She had a shaven head and strange pink glasses that looked like an extension of her pink skin. The two men wore thick beards as if to hide their faces, and held clipboards. I spent my days and nights in an EMR-machine crib looking at orange rattles.

So it went. Their funding grew, and so did I. They were careful not to retard me too much, as that would invalidate their future research. They pushed me to the limits of plasticity, then relented.

It was the deepest torture I have yet been able to imagine. They made the shifting, constantly changing world of my infant perception into an utterly unreliable, nauseatingly insecure repetition.

After orange rattles the experiments grew more advanced. They ran the 'A not B' test on me a thousand times, substituting marshmallows for toy cars for sock puppets that whispered my name. They played with my developing sense of object permanence until I trusted nothing, believed in nothing. There was no consistent reality around me. I learned to endure, and survive all the same.

"Writ/read, go high," they said to each other, as they jacked into me, a shorthand for the binary options that went through my mind.

"Writ/read, go low."

When I grew up I took that mantra for my name, not because I loved it or because I loved them, but because I used it to kill them all, and that was the first solid thing I had to rely on.

Ritry Goligh.

They plagued me with spinal punctures to tap my Cerebro-Spinal Fluid, they tested my blood, they surrounded me with the glass and metal apparatus a condemned monkey might see, as it goes to have its eyes scoured out with acid.

More tests, more scratching on paper pads, written go high, written go low, and my mind adapted to it all, but in ways they could not see. Beneath the scar tissue. Looking for a way out of the torture. It was no conscious thing, more of a defensive reaction, so that underneath their tests I built a consistent reality where I could grow.

I grew into it gradually; watching what they did to me at a slight remove, seeing how it hurt me and scarred my growing mind, and not feeling the pain or horror of it so completely.

I was insulated within the scars, and that insulation only grew thicker as their jacks grew more invasive. Perhaps they sensed something was not right, perhaps my EMR readings gave me away, but they could not punch through the defensive wall of scars my mind built for itself.

In that space, as only a child of three or four who could barely speak, who had never seen a child his own age, I began to plan. I was going to make the torture stop, and I taught myself the way to do it.

They jacked me in pairs usually, with one left behind to man the EMR, never coming in all at once. I knew I had to catch all three of them together, so I waited and prepared. I got better at sensing hints of what was coming, as their slow motions were telegraphed through the lava of my Molten Core.

Then one day I opened the wall. They fell over themselves to Jack in. More than anything, this was what they wanted. Finally, they thought, the door to forbidden knowledge had opened.

So I drew them in. I drew them deep, and once they were inside I hooked them with the Lag.

They had no chance. Where they had two pulse beats each, lazy and weak things which had never been forged and tested, I had seven tones, far stronger for all the torture they had put them through. I bound them and wrapped them up in the Lag until they had to start spitting out memories of their own just to stay alive.

The EMR powered up around me, sucking hard like a magnet, but I held them still. It was my mind, and I was the master, until finally I let them slip free. They raced for the surface, but they were too weak by then to punch through. I let their screams for help leak through.

The EMR dialed down, the world went thump-thump, and the third jacked in to the rescue.

I snatched them all. I buried them in scar tissue so deep I

couldn't even hear the screams, and that is how they died, and that is the best and worst memory of my young life.

After that things got better. It was luck, I suppose, to find a normal family, who allowed me to live a normal life. But I would never be normal again. In everything I saw, did and felt, there were echoes. Had I already done this once, like the orange rattle? My mind at its core was repetitive, unable to break out of its old patterns.

Nothing was solid. Everything was shifting. I bore the scars they had given me, the welts and weals of a thousand abuses, and though new brain-mass heaped atop that, I never felt like I truly belonged.

I finish, and now Far is looking at me with sad understanding in his eyes. I think back to the weals on his face and neck, and remember that they did this to him. They tortured him, this child-like representation of us, and he murdered them for it. This child was broken so many times that he learned to become a killer. This child is Me, too.

"I'm sorry," I tell him, even as Ray and Doe say the exact same words.

Far looks back at us with his chin quivering but jutted forth with pride.

Ray hugs him. I hug him, and Doe hugs him. We are all part of this boy, grown out of what he was. He is the heart of us, and the hardest part.

SAVE FAR

I remember the message in the mission folder. It must be true, because Far is undoubtedly the center of our chord, rooted in the primal power of the Solid Core in a way none of us can understand.

But there is little time for such comforts or revelations, as the thumping gets louder from outside and the gumball in the wall begins to shift.

RITRY GOLIGH

14. CANDYLAND

Things become a blur in the days that follow. To help me forget the look in Zachary's eyes, I drink. To help me wake up from the hangovers, I ride the ancient bonds back along the trail Mr. Ruin has left for me.

Access to the tsunami wall between Calico and Tenbridge Wulls is easy. Mr. Ruin's notes detail an ancient stop on an unbuilt Wall train line, where once they hoped to link the proto-Calico Skulks to Calico beyond. Now the station is a vacuum inside the core of the wall, locked off by great metal plugs.

Access hatches remain though. I pull up to a stretch of open wall where the night sky is brilliant with stars, and there is no walkway and there are no Skulks. I tether the speedboat to a docking ring and climb up shadowy dimples spotting the wall's flank. Soon a subglacic-like hatch appears beside me, locked by triple combination locks, and I dial in the number written down in Ruin's folder.

The chute beyond is narrow and still and smells of mold. Already I feel the thoughts of the engineers who built this place welling up from the poured concrete. These were grand dreams of a greater future, now abandoned.

I lock the hatch behind me and proceed by flashlight through a series of flood-proof doors until I emerge into an oval-framed, solitary station on an unbuilt line.

The rails have been laid and bedded with gravel, but they end in solid concrete walls at either end. A platform rises up at the side, where there are red metal seats still covered in their factory plastic. A few unpowered vending machines line the wall, interspersed between tile plates announcing this lost station's name.

ERRAL RISE

I climb to the platform, leaving trails in the thick dust as though through snowfall. The bonds here are different from the godships and the Skulks, left by scientific, detail-oriented minds driven with purpose.

Now abandoned. I sit on one of the wrapped metal seats and crack open a can of beer, one of twenty-four I brought along with a bottle of godship vodka. I set down a halogen lamp and flick the switch; it surrounds me with a globe of warm light.

I could go back to my home on Skulk 47 now, even reclaim my jack-site, but what kind of life would that be? I have started down this path into ruin, into a world of bonds and unfathomable power, and I can't stop myself now.

I drink. I see again the look in Zachary's eye as all pretence fell away and he understood who I was, and what I had come to do.

Don't hurt my children.

The memory makes me ill. Am I the man to enjoy that? I don't know. Mr. Ruin said I was a predator, but I don't want this. The Don's rheumy eyes haunt me.

I drink. I take another beer and I drink, because it is the only way I know.

Much later I walk along the tsunami wall's top, to an abandoned lighthouse. It's in the folder. They built these years ago to transmit signals out to ships on the incoming tsunami waves. There wasn't much they could say by way of warning; when you're on a tsunami wave you don't have a lot of control.

'We're sorry that you're going to die. Please try no to smash our wall.'

Crazy, pointless, but kind. I've heard stories of volunteers who patrol these places now, trying to talk down any lost souls contemplating suicide. I wonder what they might say to me, and how I would respond.

"Are you all right? Do you really want to be out here alone?"

"I'm not alone," I'd say. "I can see all the Souls of the city. I see your Soul too, and all your bonds stretching out."

"Maybe you can, but you're still alone. Here, I want to help. Will you let me? I don't want anything from you."

"Get away."

"I swear."

"Get away!"

I push him and he falls off the edge. His clothes tear off on the inclined wall, then his skin, until there is almost nothing left to hit

149

the water but bone. The rest is a long red smear stuck to the tsunami wall, like a wound in the concrete.

Another feverish dream.

I climb down and ride my stolen speedboat around the whole jagged isthmus. Skulks race by on my right and I'm just waiting for the boat to hit a hard wave and throw me out so I can drown. I am nothing good for this place. I am back where I was ten years ago, with nothing to live for at all. Mr. Ruin lied.

I don't want to be a predator. I don't want power. I don't want to cause the kind of pain I saw in Don Zachary's eyes.

The folder leads me on, to a sunken subglacic on the open ocean. If the coalitions knew it was wrecked here they would retrieve it. Ruin's guide tells me there are mindbombs aboard still. The ship is full of the dead, according to the notes. The captain was infuriated by the suspicion that his girlfriend, the first lieutenant, was sleeping with another woman, so he fired a mindbomb on his own crew that instantly Lagged their every memory and left them to die in their sinking ship.

If I dive deep enough I'll reach the airlock and be able to enter.

The thought of it intrigues me. It makes me want to go piss on the captain's rotten head. I pull up to the coordinates and toss myself into a barren stretch of gray water. It's freezing. I take a deep breath then kick down into the darkness, toward the undersea crags that clutch the subglacic like a bear's teeth closed on a fish.

I reach the hull as my flashlight sputters, shorted by the water, but never mind, the subglacic has its lights on still after all these years. Nuclear bonds go long. I grab the hatch panel and twist, it hisses open, and in I go with a rush of water. Orange lights flare and the hatch closes itself behind me, then pumps drive the water out in seconds, cycling in oxygen. The air is good but stale.

I look at the pipes and metal fittings here, gray and dreary. I have been in so many places just like this, subglacics in my own personal slice of the Arctic War.

Through the airlock I walk the metal corridors of this vessel like a ghost. This place is tilted on a diagonal, so I walk with one foot on the floor and one on the wall. The dead lie as skeletons below, like rains collecting down a river valley; here it is a river of bone, hair and uniform. All the skin is gone. My footsteps send up puffs of dust and I breathe in the old crew.

I find the captain by tracking back his jealous, raving bonds to his ready room off the bridge and I piss on his bony bald skull. I find nearby his note explaining this revenge. Perhaps he hoped one day his ship would be found, and what, future generations would sympathize with his pain?

I burn the note.

On the bridge, the sub responds to my touch. It has been lodged here for twenty years or more, a model older than mine, but it was built for the duration. I raise it to the surface and steer until the periscope is nudging up against my speedboat.

I am too drunk to be allowed to do any of this, really. I am red-eyed and beyond the reach of normal minds. I take what I need from the subglacic's munitions bay then set a dry-ice bomb on timer in the engine room and sit on the surface of the sub, just above the waves. It is like a private, temporary pier in the middle of nothing. I sit by the periscope, my elbow on its tubed lens, and sip illicit subglacic vodka brewed from CSF, recovered from the hold.

When the dry-ice bomb blows below decks, the repercussion trembles through the hull and the ship quickly begins to sink. I step into my speedboat, watching as the captain's final message of hate says goodbye forever. Thanks to me, nobody will know what he did; how he turned on his own crew and savaged them for selfishness, greed and petty jealousy. Nobody will have to find this reminder of our sad War, nobody will recover the mindbombs or dry-ice bombs or other deadly tools of our trade. They'll be forgotten and pass into legend, just like Napoleon.

That is something good I have done, I think. I stroke the bonds of the dead as they go down, as though I can offer them some comfort, drawing nothing from them. I don't want what they have to offer anymore.

The sub disappears beneath the smothering waves, a secret that will surely never be found. Bubbles rise up for a time. I tear off in my speedboat.

Around the edge of the island, I take refuge in an abandoned amusement park at the edge of a tiny town called Brink that smells of burned sugar, built beside a candy refinery. I feel myself getting fatter with every breath.

I beach the boat off the eroded blacktop parking lot and look across at the park looming against the stars. There are funfair rides here that my first batch of foster parents once took me to. I have only the dimmest memories of coming here. Perhaps I gave them to the Lag too.

By their silhouettes I identify a towering swing carousel, a gravity drop and a tall wooden roller coaster that stands still like a massive epitaph.

CANDYLAND

A faded yellow and red sign declares the name at the entrance. A tram pulls up to the station in the candy town. Two people get off then the tram pulls away again, like a yo-yo on endless repeat, headed back for Calico.

I climb over a barbed wire fence and in, over the silent parking lot. Past turnstiles I wander through this forgotten place, swollen with memories that are not my own; of families coming together and enjoying their fleeting, ephemeral lives. Perhaps I feel a little of myself here, too, as a child.

I climb the wooden roller coaster and stand at the top looking over the ruins. This is a new memory for me, now, and a new place to stand. It is a beautiful view back along the line of cities at dusk: Saunderston, Tenbridge Wulls, Calico, like hot beads of amber on a necklace.

In a hotel with a cracked façade I find an untouched room. Little packets of shampoo and conditioner remain at perfect positions in the bathroom, like marines awaiting cabin inspection. I stand at the balcony window and look out over a swimming pool that is filled with jungle, a mini-golf course succumbed to tropical bush.

"You're not who I thought you were," comes the voice from behind.

I turn, and there is Mr. Ruin. He isn't smiling anymore, he isn't smug. I still have a little strength from the last bonds I cut on Don Zachary's Skulk, and through them I feel that he is angry.

"I never was."

He stares at me. It is like staring into an empty sky and trying to resolve something of meaning, but there is nothing there. He is as lone and vengeful as the dead captain in his sub.

"I don't want to see you again," I tell him. "I don't want to know you. I don't want to even sense you've come near. You're poison. You're sick. You made a man dress up like Napoleon, for what? To get my attention? You broke Napoleon himself, and for what? Your amusement. If that's what it means to be a predator, then I am not one. I am not like you. I don't even want to remember any of this."

Mr. Ruin inclines his head. "That can be arranged."

I laugh. "Go ahead and try. They couldn't Lag me when I was a baby and they couldn't Lag me with a mindbomb, so what do you think you're going to do? You're not a shark, you're a spider, and I'll crush you underfoot."

Now he smiles. Those gleaming white teeth shine like bulls' eyes in the dark.

"Ritry, I am so glad you've said these things. It will make it much easier, when the time comes. I'd always hoped to sample a seven-toned soul, and now you're offering me the chance."

I take a step forward. "Try it. Jack all you want. I'll drown you in your own fucking mind."

He laughs. "Oh, no. Do you really think I would come at you so directly, when you've just said I'm a spider? Ritry, you are so right, and I will savor this. Your fall will be long, and low, and hard. I will grind all the juice out of you like I did Napoleon, and at the end you'll still jack the Solid Core for me, because I'm strong and you are not. When that day comes, remember what you said here. Remember your arrogance in the face of things you can not possibly understand, and remember that you did it to yourself."

"I'm not afraid of you," I say. "You're a coward."

He sighs, and I feel something different in him despite everything he says. Sadness. Loneliness, stretching out like the empty Arctic waters. "No. I'm just hungry, and bored. But I have forever, and nobody will stop me." I catch waves of regret ebbing out like a tide. "Ah, we would've had such times, Ritry, you and I. You've given up so much. But no matter, I have all the time in the world. I'll come for you when you're ready. We'll ride together at the last, whether you want to or not."

Then he is gone.

I think about chasing him, taking the fight to him and killing him now like I've killed before, but I am too tired. I don't want to hurt people anymore. Besides, I'll be ready.

I slump onto the bed and a cloud of dust whuffs up around me. I feel light and not drunk enough. There are tiny bottles of liquor in the fridge.

I drink them all.

The world is different when I wake. The last strength of the bonds I cut on Don Zachary's Skulk has gone, and what remains is only the swell of nostalgia, love and happy memories rising off the park.

I rise and throw back the curtains to a golden dawn, falling on the jungle and ocean beyond like manna, a heavenly glow so bright I have to shade my eyes.

I have been a thing of the night for so long. I have fought and jacked and screwed and hustled in the grime, and I am tired of it. I have lived on a floating platform waiting every day for a tsunami to come, big enough to rub me out completely and wash all trace of my existence away.

But enough. The taste of these past ten years is sour in my mouth. That could be the liquor, but it's also the past. It tastes foul and I spit it out. I scrape my tongue with my sleeves and rub the fabric around my teeth.

I want to be clean.

The glow in the park fades, but it is still alive. The trees sway in the sea breeze. The bushes fluff out seeds, ever hopeful, seeking a solid place to sink into and grow. I feel like a seed that has been drifting for thirty-five years, waiting for the moment to put down roots and reach for the sun.

So I let it go. I drop it all in that room, along with the alcohol, the bonds and the dark promise of Mr. Ruin. I don't need it now. I'm ready to begin again.

ME

K. CALICO

Doe kicks out the gumball with a loud schlock and we pour sinuously into another pulsing tunnel. The worms are on us at once and I toss out fragments of our ancient past like dry-ice grenades as we run; they burst but other worms replace them, while every piece of ammo is a memory permanently lost, trading mass for speed.

"Incoming!" Ray cries, and fires one variation of the orange rattle.

We run, we turn, we run.

"Incoming!" Doe cries and hurls out first family with enough force to tear a gaping hole in the maze itself. So's route abruptly shifts in my HUD, guiding us through the ruptured organic tear into another room where another book lies, but I don't need to read it because now I remember it all.

CALICO

I go to Calico.

It's a surprisingly easy thing, crossing this barrier I've built in my mind for so long. A tsunami wall always stood in the way, but nobody forced me onto the Skulk-side. I didn't commit any crime, I wasn't banished there; I just exiled myself.

Standing in Calico Central station, beside the wall-top train line that carried me from the little town of Brink, I look over this city that comprises the last of humanity. Fifty years ago all this was a slim mountain range hidden by ice; then the ice was blasted away in the resource wars, the waters rose, and it became a foundation for that remains of humanity. Anywhere near the equator is a burning inferno of sand and tornados. Much of the northern climes are inundated with meltwater and battered by storms.

Only here in the Arctic Circle can we really endure.

Calico rises before me in skyscrapers of glass and steel. Neon lights race up and down their teetering flanks. There are parks and highways, libraries and a stadium. While the dregs in proto-Calico lapped up their shark arenas and brothels and waited for the final tsunami to come rub them out, Calico has been growing.

It is beautiful to see this much hope. These people still believe there is a future, and it brings tears to my eyes. I can feel them dimly through my remnant strength in the bonds. Here they follow laws, and get promotions, and raise families. Here they work their way up the hierarchy, and marry, and it is so different from proto-Calico that I can almost not bear it.

I always used to think that these people were the ones lying to themselves. The inhabitants of the Skulks were the only ones seeing clearly. Now I see that the people in the Skulks have just given up. I was one of them for the longest time. I think back on my ten years at the jack-site, drinking to shut up the voices in my head, jacking minds to drown the guilt in my own.

I can see it clearly now; if a new world will come from anywhere, it is from Calico, and I want to be part of it. I've had enough of despair. If Mr. Ruin has taught me anything, it is that some people are worth saving.

I descend into Calico. They check my records and admit me with a smile. I'm a kind of hero here, I suppose, one of the few Soul Jackers to survive the war. I walk into streets that are clean and shiny with fresh rain. You don't see the boundless, hopeless gray of the ocean here, ever-threatening to rise up and crush you. You just see other people; the things that people built and are building.

This place is alive. The air fills my lungs like never before.

I track down Carrolla. At least three months have passed since our encounter with the Don. Through the sense of him in the bonds, I find the hospital he was admitted to, then the apartment he took and the job he found.

It's a bar near the wall. He's working on the counter when I walk in, favoring his hand with its fingers re-attached. The place is nothing like the bars of the Skulks, built out of flotsam. Everything here is sheer and shiny, clean and new, with fake bleach pine and brushed chrome.

Soul Jacker

I stand in front of him. He looks at me for a long moment before he realizes who I am. Then he gasps.

"What in the hell? Rit. What are you doing here?"

I look at his hand on the bar. You can hardly see the scars; tiny suture lines at the knuckle. He pulls it away as if ashamed. His teeth set tightly and he pales a little.

"I know you're angry," I say. "I would be too. But I want you to know Don Zachary will never come looking for you."

He studies me. I can feel his disbelief. That I'm here, that I'm telling the truth. He eyes the door nervously. Probably he thinks I've sold him out? But what sense would that make, when the Don only wanted me?

"Did you kill him?" he asks.

"No. I Lagged him."

He stares at me. "You Lagged the Don? How? How would you even get close?"

I shrug. The moment cracks open, and he starts to laugh. "Ritry goddamned Goligh. You are one crazy son of a bitch."

I smile. "How are your fingers?"

He flips me off. A moment passes. We are not in the Skulks anymore. Whatever we had before isn't the same over here. There's something still, but it's weak, and soon it will be gone.

That's OK.

"They have Arcloberry here?" I ask.

He grins. "Not here. But we'll find some."

We walk out like that, big model-looking Carrolla dressed in his bar bowtie, me in a sharp black suit, and find another bar. We toast each other and everything we've achieved, in escaping the Skulks. It's a good night, and the last of its kind.

I sleep that night in a business hotel designed for travelers come from the neighboring cities on the Calico range; Tenbridge Wulls and Saunderston. It's high up and has a great view of the wall, peeking over the lip to the endless gray beyond. It is strange to feel protected, for once. My War built all of this, and I deserve to feel safe.

I check my accounts. Money has been piling up in them for years: interest from the pay-off I got after quitting active coalition service and money I put aside from the jack-site. There was nothing to spend it on in the Skulks.

I go to sleep thinking about Carrolla. I don't expect to see him again.

Days pass in peace. I find an apartment near the high-class Reach, with a view of the city. I don't want to see the water any more. I walk. Calico is calm, safe, and restful. People go where they go and do what they do bound by clear, clean laws. I reflect on this collation détente we have arrived at. It only took the destruction of the world to reach it.

I stand in a park and look up at he towers of the Reach; they are vast, soaring into the sky, and I am now at the bottom of them all, but I am glad of it. Thirty-seven years old, and I have a new start. Within a month I find work as a licensed Soul Jacker's assistant in a low-floored lab, where none of the technicians are ex-marines, where sex never precedes or follows an implantation, and where they never jack deeper than the outer boundary of security their technology can provide against the Lag.

There is no risk. Instead of the natural massage of sex as a balm after the rough process of memory injection, they administer artificial chemical cocktails so expertly constructed and fine-tuned to the host that the mind barely notices the difference. Even so, the process still requires a warm and relaxed human touch, making a good bedside manner essential. I have that. For the rest, I tuck my chin in and my head down and do the work.

For one year I man a sonic basin, trusted only to stand nearby while the patients watch colorful displays thrum their pulse back at them through audio and visual displays. I don't socialize much, though I go to meetings for recovering alcoholics. I don't drink.

A year in they promote me to administering Cerebro-Spinal Fluid, the liquid that bathes and cools the brain. I study hard at nights, learning their rules and the new and proper way to jack the mind. I earn all the certificates I can, by far the oldest student in all my night classes, and within two years am manning the EMR and preparing syringes of silvery engrams to inject.

It takes three years in all before they let me lead a jack. It feels like returning to an old friend. They are all watching, my new colleagues and workmates, many of them younger than me, more educated than me, kids from the Reach and partners from the firm, waiting to see if I choke.

Will I jack too deep and go organic, back to my old way of the Skulks? Will I panic and regress, forcing the machine into damage control?

They don't know me at all. I jack the brain like a virtuoso conductor, using all the tricks and techniques I'd learned before in concert with the new technology. The patient says afterward it was the smoothest engram he'd ever received, so seamless and integrated he couldn't distinguish it from his real knowledge. He tells me all this in fluent Hexi-Canton, the language engram I implanted.

I do it in the fastest time anyone in my jack-site has seen. Soon the partners are knocking on the door of my office to ask me how I did it. I tell them what I can, what I am able to put into words. I am a giver now, not a taker.

One day the tsunami comes.

It's a big one, enough to toss a few of the Skulks up and over the wall itself, crushing the rest under thirty feet of water. Nobody in Calico is hurt, because we are ready, though everyone on the Skulks will be dead. Everyone I once knew, rubbed out, except perhaps Don Zachary in his underwater bunker.

My new life goes on. I meet a woman called Loralena, of proto-Rusk stock. She is nothing like the women of my past, or any of the girls from the Skulks. She is utterly self-possessed, in control of her emotions and heart but still alive in every moment.

She is an artist of some medium fame, who specializes in painting with information from the brain. She takes Cerebro-Spinal Fluid samples and EMR brainscans from famous politicans, businesspeople and artists and extrapolates the resulting data into vast, riotous tableaux of color. I meet her at a Soul Jacker party for funders, when one of the partners introduces us.

"You should sample Ritry," he says. "He's a complete mystery. Perhaps you'll get back to us with the inside scoop on how he does what he does."

Polite laughter, he nudges my shoulder, and I smile.

"I'd love to," she says. "Ritry, when will you come by?"

I make some polite hemming and hawing about soon, and I'd be delighted. We move on to talk about the Skulks, and she espouses her theories on re-absorption, about how everything that dies doesn't really die but gets taken up again in a different way. It doesn't matter if it's matter, energy, or thought, which she said was a kind of energy itself.

"It all comes around," she says with vivacious light in her eyes. "It all circulates."

She is stunning, for how alive she is. When she isn't speaking she listens intently, and sips on her ancient-genome rye and ice. I can feel that she is hoovering all this up, not just the words and the tastes but the mood, every single tiny gesture. She is three years my junior, has curly auburn hair that makes me think of summers that I never saw, and radiates a fierce wonder and curiosity about everything that lights me up inside.

I go to her studio the next day for the sample, in the lower hills of the Rise. It is large and white on the outside, amongst a hillscape of large white villas. Inside the walls are slashed everywhere with her strange art; blown-up mathematical equations, genetic coding strips, a mad variety of patterning types, even some sculptures that somehow represent the helical DNA.

"They say you're a dark horse," she says, as I lay back on the EMR chair so she can take a reading. "Are you sure you want me to expose all your secrets?"

I smile. "I'd like to see them made into something beautiful."

She gives me a long, thoughtful look. "I'll do my best."

We are both mostly business-like. I flirt a little about her hair, she flirts a very little about my build, which I've kept up since my marine days. It is very pleasant and slightly distant, and after the scan she deftly turns down my suggestion of a date to an art museum in the Reach on my way out. I consider it finished.

Soul Jacker

Time passes. I occupy my off-hours wandering the city, enjoying the feel of the solid earth under my feet. I like looking up at the towers, imagining how high they might one day grow, perhaps even tall enough to outrace the gathering tides. When I feel low I climb the wall and walk along it too, looking down on the dirty blue Skulks as they pull themselves back up out of the water. By night they buzz with neon arteries like my old alley, trafficked by money and Souls coming in, money and Souls going out.

Don Zachary's bunker is still there, a foundation stone for the Skulks as ever, and I wonder about that life; to be the only solid thing amidst gossamer threads. Does it make him feel better, superior, like Mr. Ruin?

Whenever I think about Ruin, I turn my mind to something else. At some point I hear that Carrolla has returned to the Skulks, so I imagine the wild life he is living down there. Maybe he's finally running his bar of subglacic parts. I think back on my old life but I don't hanker for it.

Three months later Loralena calls, though I never gave her my number. She invites me to see her latest work, saying she's finally finished working my data. It is in her studio, so I go. She meets me at the entrance with the fire of curiosity burning in her eyes.

"Who are you, Ritry Goligh?" she asks.

I shrug. "Soul Jacker. Art appreciator. Wall-hiker."

"And so much more," she says, and leads me through.

The painting of my mind is bigger than any of the others. It covers the floor and the walls both, so immense are the patterns and the details within it. It is a maze of seven distinct parts, with each part completely different from the others, represented in a different way.

Seven tones.

She takes my arm in her own. "I've never seen anything like it. I want to know everything about you."

Despite myself, I choke up a little. I wait for it to subside before I answer. "Would you care to walk the wall with me?"

We walk the wall. I talk a little, revealing brief hints of who I was and have been, but each time only in exchange for something from her.

I learn that she grew up sheltered from the dying years of the war, tucked deep away in an oasis holdout somewhere in the midst of the old neo-Armorica desert belt, far from the suprarene tank routes.

Her parents had been climatologists, and every day since she was a small girl they'd taken her out to walk the dunes encroaching the tops of old skyscrapers; buried cities that had once been the heart of the world.

"Imagine this," they always told her, "imagine how it was for them, and how it will be for us in a thousand years."

They taught her the long perspective of ice ages and extinction-level events, about the tumbling of sand particles in the air as water was sucked out of soil and into the oceans. They asked her to imagine divinity as a circle, not a religion in a book; a circle that goes round and round and never stops remaking itself.

I love to hear her stories. She loves to hear mine. One night we walk the wall so far we come to the old lighthouse I'd almost jumped from, and I start to cry.

She takes my chin in her hand, my sadness matched in her own eyes, and says, "Tell me, Ritry. Please."

So I do. I tell her all of it, in bits and pieces. She weeps for me, at times. She laughs with me. I share it all.

We sleep together for the first time in that lighthouse, surrounded by the bonds of people who'd dreamed of offering succor to those who were going to die.

"I want to see it," she says, in the morning that followed. "The place that made you change. At the end of the line."

I take her there, back to Candyland. It is a little more ruined now, a little more overgrown, though the thick scent of burning sugar from the sweets factory still fills the air. I find the room where I'd faced down Mr. Ruin. It is wrecked in a way I don't remember from before, strewn with bottles. Loralena picks up one and studies the brand; vodka from the subglacic I sank. She picks up another, from the godships.

Soul Jacker

She looks at me and nods.

"I'm so proud of you right now."

We walk the dried-out riverbeds of the Ragin' River donut loop. We climb the heights of the wooden roller coaster. Sitting huddled together at the top, wrapped up in a blanket borrowed from the ruined hotel, we look back over the dusk falling over the pearly string of Calico cities.

"I was raped once," she tells me. I listen. She goes on to tell me how, and who it was. A client from her early days as an artist, who thought the passion he felt for her was requited. It wasn't, so he took it. He since fled to the Skulks, and died in the last tsunami.

I hold her, and she holds me. It is a start, building real roots in that forgotten place.

The best times of my life follow. I become senior partner at the jack-site. Loralena goes on to publish amazing works, though she never shares the one drawn from my mind with anyone else. Together we fold it up and burn it over a glass of ancient-genome rye.

"To the future," we toast.

Our first child comes a year later. We call her Art, after our shared passion. A year later comes a boy, whom we name Memory, Mem for short. We spoil them in everything, and take them everywhere. We walk the wall and made up games for counting all the ships out at sea, we plan elaborate treasure hunts across the length and breadth of Calico to keep them guessing and giggling, we play in the ruins of Candyland building makeshift towers out of chairs and tables. We make a thousand new memories together, with a thousand more to come, and they bring a real depth and meaning to a life I'd always lived for myself. It's something I never thought I wanted, but I love it with a passion fiercer than I've ever felt before.

Then comes Mr. Ruin.

"It's him," says Far, pointing at the name in the last line, on the last page. "He's done this to us."

I know it. I remember how he boasted of the tortures of Napoleon, and I remember the Napoleonic soldiers clustered about the Deathgate.

"He put them there," Far says, "to lock us in." We all turn to him. I've never heard him speak like this, with this confidence. His teeth are gritted. He looks angry, like a child who could bury three people in his own Soul.

"He wants the Core," I say.

"He wants the power," Far says.

There's no need to explain any further, because I see it now; beyond the Solid Core lies enough power to upend Ritry Goligh's world and enslave every last Soul alive.

We cannot let that happen.

A worm's head smashes through the wall and Ray fires all our memories of Mem into it. The worm dissolves like a QC particle has disrupted it, but now we have lost-

Someone.

"Arm yourself," I shout as the thunder of galloping worms draws in; the final storm. We muster pieces of the recent past and rip through the wall like one fluid, organic motion, knowing instinctively who will take the lead; Doe, then Ray, then Me, then Far to bring up the rear.

This is the way it has to be. We race down tunnels leaving explosions in our wake, spending this precious currency we have just gained, losing who we were and what we've done in pursuit of the core directive we wrote for ourselves.

Save Ritry Goligh.

RITRY GOLIGH

15. TREASURE HUNT

It's a treasure hunt day.

The clues to the hunt are hidden in Loralena's latest work of art; a number of impossible creatures enfolded within its colors and patterns. There's a porpoise-finned dog and a monkey with tentacle limbs, a clamshell mouse and an elephant-whale.

We spent a merry evening a week earlier sketching them, while the children were asleep. In the drawing room of our 50th floor apartment in Calico Reach, drinking good red ice-wine and looking out over the city's pulsing neon lights, we grew increasingly tipsy and our sketches grew more outlandish.

"Your anemone looks like a football," Loralena teased. "A fat football with a thousand fat legs."

"It's not even an anemone," I said, a little giddy. "It's a universe in bloom."

She leaned on my shoulder with her arm around my back, squinting at my artistic effort. I kissed the soft curve of her neck and tasted the faint residue of her perfume; an anniversary gift.

"What kind of universe blooms in the Arctic?" she asked, nonplussed. "Are you quite mad?"

I laughed. "You saw my brain. You married me."

She chuckled and wriggled over the chair arm to sit in my lap. She tapped the drawing. "I hate to say it, but this particular protuberance looks sexual."

"That's the spiral arm. Or maybe it's a seahorse tail?"

Another kiss, some more snuggling. Rooting underneath her, she found something in my lap that seemed to amuse her.

"That's not part of the treasure hunt," I said, and she smirked.

"That depends what hunt I'm on. Right now I'm hunting for impossibly small things, and I think I found one."

"And oh look," I said, my hands rising to cup her breasts. "I found two. Does that make me the winner?"

She leaned closer, whispered, "Silly," in my ear and kissed me harder. She tasted of sweet wine and happiness. I carried her to bed and the treasure hunt continued. I didn't know then that it would be the last time.

The treasure hunt begins at breakfast.

We give the kids the map and instantly they are transfixed; scanning and deciphering. They catch on to the sea animal-theme quickly, and soon lead us out of the apartment at a run.

"We'll do the sea-dog first, then go catch some fish," Art suggests and Mem agrees, in the elevator heading down. In the lobby they race away and we wave them off; already forgotten. There is a record to beat.

Loralena and I laugh as we wander down to the park, where we spend most of the day lazing in the grass, following their progress on our nodes; little blinking lights that rack up points as they go.

We read books, dabble our feet in the fountain, and talk about the next hunt we'll plan. I have so many ideas. When the kids come back we tally the points and pay up. Mem spends all her earnings on new games. Art teases her and only spends a quarter on a new painting easel, something he's taking after her mother in. We put them to bed exhausted and happy. I go to sleep with Loralena in my arms; the last perfect night of my new perfect life.

When I wake, I know he's come. I feel it in the air, a disturbance of the faint bonds of my dreams.

Mr. Ruin.

I look at the clock; 3am. The digits cast a green glow, making the cream bedroom walls sickly. Loralena's sleeping beside me and the kids are in the room next door, and suddenly it all feels so fragile, like fine bone china that will crack if I make one wrong move.

But I've been waiting for this moment for ten years. I'm ready. I get out of bed and go to find him. In the hallway I can tell from the open door that he's in the childrens' room. The sharp chill of fear thrills down my spine, and a swell of fury rises to meet it.

The door creaks as I enter. The carpet is soft under my bare feet. He stands between Art and Mem as they sleep in their beds. He's wearing the same gray suit, the same Napoleonic hat. His teeth shine as white as the first time I saw him in the shark-fighting arena.

"Hello, Ritry," he says, grinning as ever. "You've been busy. Lucky for me, I suppose."

Without saying a word of warning I activate the mindbomb.

I stole it from the sunken subglacic ten years ago; a heavy gray tube pried out of the missile-loading bay. I wired it into the house and programmed its destructive frequencies to shield the Souls of my family. I set the detonation pattern to a thought triggered over the bonds, and ensured the walls and ceiling of our apartment were sufficiently insulated to contain it.

The bomb explodes and the shockwave buzzes over me like hard static electricity, rebounding back off the insulated walls and swamping Mr. Ruin in the middle.

He drops flat to the floor. I drop to my knees under the onslaught. Ten, fifteen pass as the last reverberations rattle back and forth in the echo chamber I've made.

Then there is silence; only the soothing sound of Art and Mem sleeping. They'll have bad dreams, but that's nothing compared to what the mindbombs were designed for. I push myself to my feet, looking down at Mr. Ruin lying flat on the carpet. My heart throbs hard as the shock of what I've done hits me. He's dead; his mind erased.

Then he moves. My heart skips a beat and all feeling drains from my body as control is taken away. Lagged.

Mr. Ruin stands up. It is impossible, he should be as dead now as Ven and Heclan, but he is not. On his feet now, he dusts down his jacket and looks at me with an expression approaching remorse. "Anything else, Ritry?"

I send the signal to detonate the bomb again, but of course it is spent. I try once more to be sure, because now there is nothing else I can do. The shock of my victory gives way to an all-pervading terror. He is here in my house. He is standing between my children. He survived a mindbomb?

I try to charge him but he Lags the weight of my intent away with ease, as though I am a weakling child, and my body does no more than lean slightly forward. The strength he can muster is awesome and I can do nothing underneath it but tremble.

"Oh, Ritry," he says, disappointment in his voice. "I do feel badly about this part. But dear boy, who do you think gave you the location of that subglacic? It was me, wasn't it? Everything you've got and everything you've made of yourself is because of me." He nods gently, agreeing with himself. "You see that now, don't you?"

I realize then how thoroughly I have lost. In a second I have lost everything, and now I am helpless. I am Don Zachary lying in his opulent bed, able only to beg for the lives of my children. A cold emptiness hollows me out and squats like a solid lump in the center of my gut, thick and curdled and impossible to ignore.

I am prey.

My throat tries to gag. I realize with sudden certainty that I should never have allowed myself to love Loralena, should never have allowed myself to have children. I was arrogant and a fool to believe one mindbomb would be enough, and now I am going to pay. I want to sag to the carpet and vomit all of this up, but Ruin doesn't let me move. I want to close my eyes and wake from a nightmare but I can't do anything, can't move, can't fight, can't even close my eyes.

Tears stream down my cheeks.

"Ah," says Mr. Ruin, his voice transcendent, like this is the most beautiful thing he's ever witnessed. "At last you see who I am."

I gather what strength I have to bark a single word. "How?"

His smile is sympathetic. "You only took one bomb, correct? Yes." He takes off the Napoleonic hat and turns it so I can see the interior. Inside there are winking lights on a machine built around the brim. Now I can hear the tinny little thump thump of the electromagnets doing their work; smaller than I've ever seen before.

A portable EMR. A shield.

I almost laugh. He prepared. All of this has been his trap.

"I will kill you," I manage to say through gritted teeth.

"I've heard that before. You had your chance. Now it's my turn." He reaches down to stroke Mem's sleeping head. I try to scream but I can't make a sound. "Look around you, Ritry. Wouldn't you say this is fair compensation for all that I gave you? Isn't it only just I take my share? And what's to stop me? I could Lag your whole fucking family and drop myself in your place in a heartbeat." He snaps his fingers, the sound obscenely loud in the quiet room. "Did you ever think of that?"

The lump in my stomach only gets harder, thicker, sicker; so repellent I can scarcely breathe.

"I could be fucking your wife, Ritry," he whispers conspiratorially. "Your beautiful painter wife, and she'll call out your name while I do it. How would you feel about that? Your kids will call me papa. Art and Mem, what kind of names are those anyway? We'll change that. And do you know the best thing? Nobody but you and I will know. They say Job had it bad. Ritry, I'll make it so you never existed."

I gasp. A second flood of tears mists my eyes.

"Come now, be reasonable," he says. "You must know you owe all this to me. When I first found you you were despondent, only waiting to die. I gave you the world and you turned me down, but you kept everything else, and how is that fair? I'm only here to claim my due, and put you back where you belong. You were nothing then, and so you would have stayed. Don't look at me like that, Ritry. Ask yourself, is this what I, Mr. Ruin, wanted? I didn't want this. I wanted you at my side, a partner in the great mission to jack the Solid Core, but you rejected me. I can't allow that to stand."

"Please," I manage to whisper.

He laughs. "That's a beginning. Perhaps in ten years? In twenty? I might relent. But until then, I need you to understand. You take your punishment like a good boy. You don't try to end it prematurely, because if you die then so do they. You don't Lag the memories or the pain away, because if you do they'll die. You don't even try to jack for the Core, not until I say so, because first you have to pay for your crimes. If you do anything other than roll belly-up and take it until I say it's enough, they all die."

More tears come, so thick I can barely see. If I had control of my body I'd be gasping.

Ruin nods appreciatively. "Good. Now, to a point of order. You said before that I couldn't break your mind, and maybe you were right. There's just too much scar tissue built up inside. But them?"

He nods to my children. I want to tear out his eyes. I want to drop on my knees and beg for forgiveness.

"There's nothing special about them."

I let out a sob. The misery is already too strong for him to Lag.

He notices. "That's more like it. Come on, Ritry, let me hear you bawl. Didn't I say it would come to this? You poor child, didn't I warn you? I gave you everything and you threw it back in my face, and now you're going to pay."

I push back with all the strength I can muster, and speak. "Kill me."

He looks pleasantly surprised.

"Really? Do you know, that is exactly what Napoleon said to me? When I told him what awaited him, alone on a stinking hole of an island to while away his piss-ant life in ignominy and dishonor, unable to even kill himself, that is exactly what he said. And do you know what I said to him?"

He leaves this hanging. I am only standing now because he wants me to.

"I told him, where would be the fun in that?" His eyes glow hot. "But alive? Ritry, I'll feast on this for as long as you live. Have you any idea the strength I'm going to get from your misery? You're a seven-toned freak, and breaking those bonds is going to be a-fucking-tomic. You will be my masterpiece. I fitted you for a suit and for the past ten years you've put it on, piece by piece, and I've watched. Gods, how I've watched and waited. Every delicious kiss, every touch on your children's hair, every kind word, every bit of it gone!"

He is red-faced now, working himself up, and I am shrinking down to a sick little nothing deep inside myself, full of shame and disgrace. "You put the suit on for me, Ritry. You did it by yourself, and you thought it was a rebellion." His smile widens, his eyes shine with happiness. "Then when the time is right, you will jack the Core for me. You will find the bridge to beyond." He pauses, perhaps overcome with his own victory. "Really, it's too much, Ritry. And you once had the gall to threaten me? Who's the predator now, you fucking idiot, who's the true shark?"

He lets his grip on me loosen. I can barely breathe, barely move, but I can speak.

"Say it," he says impatiently. "Come on, spit it out."

I know what he wants; he'll have read it in my Soul as I now read it in his. I am Don Zachary fallen to nothing. I give it to him.

"Please don't hurt my children."

He laughs. "I'll do whatever I want."

16. NEW MAN

He banishes me to the Skulks, and there I drink. I cannot drink enough. I drink until I vomit and pass out, then I drink some more.

Still I dream. There can be no escape. I cry and groan, I roll around in the filth and dirt of a new floating park on a new Skulk in a new proto-Calico, gnashing my teeth and covering myself in ashes.

I beg and I wail at the skies until the locals come and beat the frustration out of me, then I huddle in a freezing ball and whine, blood running down my burst lips and chest, as I feel every bit of everything Mr. Ruin does.

My family forget me. They forget every piece of me, and just like he said, he takes my place.

"I'm sorry!" I shout up at the sky, "please, I'm so sorry."

He does fuck my wife. He does change the names of my children. He treats them like shit and he makes them think it was me, then Lags the weight of it away so they never realize and can never escape, and he does it all over again. He turns the love we had inside out and feeds off the pain.

No one can help me. There's nothing I can do but drink, so I drink. When the locals come to beat me I don't fight, I only keep myself alive.

My ribs break, and I drink a hundred bottles of Arcloberry. My fingers break, and I drink all the gene-spliced rye in the world. My teeth break, and I drink all the rum. My hair grows long and shaggy, I stink, I'm wearing whatever ragged clothes I can scrabble for and I weep or whisper every night, begging him to let it end.

It doesn't end.

He twists the things we used to do to make them awful; treasure hunts purloined to torture. He beats them. He torments them. He breaks them, and they weep too, and beg, and he Lags it away to begin again.

I can do nothing but drink and sob and break my body on the rack.

A year passes.

Skulk 12. The pain is numb but always there. I wake with the pain and I sleep with it. When I'm lucky, when I can steal it or beg it, I drink. Some of my fingers don't work as well as they used to. It's not as bad as it was, almost tolerable, but there are always spikes.

He left my family, mostly, but he goes back. They live a normal life for weeks at a time, missing me, until he gets hungry and goes back to dine. He has his favored tortures perfected to a routine, which he always Lags at the end. He tells them these are business trips he goes on, and every time they wait for him like they would wait for me, eager and ready. Every time he comes back and he hurts them, and every time it is just as bad. Unlike me, they can never get used to it.

I am inured. I still sob and drink when they're in the thick of it, but in the between times, when they miss me but not too much, there is some relief.

I share the park with another homeless man. He hunts crull using complex traps, just like the marine from before. We watch each other warily across the fake grass of this sad, sagging park and I wonder if he is the same man I once waved to. Hours I spend wondering this, as though the answer will solve something or help in any way.

He eyes me back. Perhaps he wonders if I am the same Ritry Goligh who once looked at him from my apartment window, Soul Jacker to Skulk 47. But this is not Skulk 47; it is Skulk 12, after the tsunami came.

I saw Carrolla once, I think. I was roaming this Skulk's back-alleys scrounging for liquor to steal, like a sickly ghast, and I saw him. He was noisy, happy, walking with a woman on his arm and talking loudly about his restaurant.

It had to be Carrolla, but wasn't he planning a bar? I wondered if he remembered me fondly. Did he ever think of our days together?

Night comes, and I've spent another day staring into space, waiting for the wounds in my mind to heal. I feel like less and less every day, like I've forgotten something I ought to know and my mind is hiving off into constituent parts. Perhaps I'm forgetting who I am, or perhaps this is madness.

Maybe it will be a relief.

The marine across the way has been roasting crull for an hour. The seaweed newsprint he rolls it in smells like burning hair. He wears rags like me. I wonder if a subglacic suit would fit him anymore, or how he might look holding a Kaos rifle as he attacks a hydrate base atop the ice.

He waves. Perhaps he has liquor. I roll to my feet and trudge across the park. The barrels underfoot list and bob. Everything is falling apart. Soon there'll be a lake here, and soon there'll be another tsunami, and soon we'll all be wiped clean.

Napoleon, I think. Napoleon on Elba.

I grunt as I draw near. By firelight he looks filthy, his face grimed with old sweat. He hawks and spits.

"It never gets easier," he says. His voice sounds like sandpaper on chalkboard, deep and abrading and mottled with phlegm. Probably tuberculosis.

These are our first words after a year, but the meaning is clear. I know him as he knows me. We are the same in some way.

He hands me a jar of clear liquid and I take it eagerly, knock back a heavy swig. It is sharply acidic, perhaps some kind of medical cleaner. It strips the feeling from my tongue and throat and blooms heat in my stomach. Every bit of it helps to dispel the cold, if only for a little while.

They miss me, I feel. They think I'm coming back.

"It's good," I manage, shuffling close to his fire. It's cool out now, perhaps it's winter. I barely notice anymore.

He shrugs. "Finish it. Stole it from the Soul Jacker."

I laugh. I look again at the jar and recognize it. It's got a CSF label, fermented from a Soul Jacker's Cerebro-Spinal Fluid. For a moment I'm back with Heclan, Ferrily and Tigrates on the subglacic again in the midst of the War, distilling in secret and slowly drawing closer to Ven.

Past lives, almost forgotten. I finish it in hungry gulps. The fumes burn up my nose and make my eyes water. When I'm done I sway.

"Sit," he says. I sit.

He pulls a chunk of crull apart and hands a wing to me. It is greasy and brown, spotted in places with feather stubs. I realize I am famished; how long since I last ate? I tear into the meat and swallow it in gristly chunks with juices running down my chin.

"I knew it was you," the man says.

I look at him and see that he is indeed the same man. I nod. I wonder how he survived the tsunami, or if I've somehow slipped back in time to that old park on 47, and just across the way is another me in another life, behind a kind of glass I can never break.

Memory. We're always looking in from the outside.

We eat, and he produces another jar of fermented CSF. We sip it and the world swirls pleasantly. As ever, I begin to forget. Leaning back to watch the stars, I wonder which Ritry Goligh I really am. Am I the boy who had no parents, or the marine who lost his crew, or the man who told Don Zachary what to do and lived, or the man who lost it all?

Am I Napoleon himself?

"Come on," the ex-marine says. His face is lined and haggard, but there's something like brotherhood in his eyes. He's pointing to his hut, hidden amidst the poles and floating trees, built out of blue tarp like a tent. "Let me show you."

I don't care. If he wants to screw me, let him try. I'll either kill him or let him, and either way it'll be a kind of forgetting.

"It's OK," he says. "I know."

On my knees, moving in a blur, I crawl through the bushes to his home. I kneel before the opening and he pulls the sheet wall aside.

There is a lamp glowing within, illuminating a small cave-like space that looks like a shrine. It dizzies me. The canvas walls are covered in old photographs, taped and tacked into place. There are bits of faded yellow paper with childlike drawings on them; crayon outlines delineating a house, a tree, a mother and father and two girls.

In the photographs I see his two daughters and his wife. He is dressed as a marine, standing by her side in their wedding clothes in front of some shiny Calico church. They are happy and smiling and proud. I look around the shrine and see his family everywhere, covering every surface so the blue tarp beneath looks like lines of mortar in a structure built of memory. Scattered around the floor are numerous items; a small and singed teddy bear, a pack of plastic toy marines, child's clothes.

It is a tangle of bonds so hot I can feel it buoying me up, with every one pointing at the man standing behind me. Tears well into my eyes; for the first time in a year not for my own suffering, but for the suffering of another.

I turn and see him standing there, tears in his eyes too.

"It doesn't make it easier," he says, pointing at the shrine. "But it helps."

I nod and rub the tears away.

"Thank you," I say and lurch to my feet. "Thank you."

Staggering away, I feel some part of me change. The part that has been shearing off for months, a part that I once hid behind a wall made of my own scar tissue, begins to plan, and I give over control to it. For the first time in a year I sense a sliver of hope in the darkness. I don't know why and I don't know how, but I know what I have to do.

17. THE REACH

I go at once. Drunk and stinking, dressed only in rags, I cross the wall into Calico. People stare at me as I ride the Wall line to the Reach. They step away and turn up their noses, and I do not blame them. I need this. A man in a suit with a briefcase jostles me hard to my knees. When I drop, he uses the case to hit me in the face.

My nose breaks. That's OK.

Mr. Ruin feels me coming, and he tightens his noose of control around my family's throats. It's a risk, but the only thing I can do.

Nobody stops me as I walk into my old building. I ride the elevator in silence, halfway between terror and elation. I might see them again. I might get them all killed.

The door is ajar and I walk in. It is my old home. Loralena is standing in the middle of the room with Mem and Art either side of her. They have grown so much. When they see me the hope in their eyes peaks, then sinks as he Lags them.

He emerges from the kitchen. Ruin in all his gray, white-toothed glory. My master. "I told you never to come here, Ritry," he says.

"I just need," I begin, but I am so drunk and my nose so broken I can't speak well.

"You are disgusting," he says. "What is it? Here, let me."

He leaps the bonds between us, into my mind. I have a little strength now, but not nearly enough. The power he's raised from Lagging them, from feeding off me even now, makes me useless to resist.

He reads the marine's tent shrine, and grins his big white grin. "You want mementos," he says. "Well, of course, Ritry. Of course. Take a seat."

I take a seat right there, in the doorway, on the floor.

"Very good," he says. "Now wait."

I sit and look at my wife. She is pale and fresh worry lines wrinkle her face, but she is my Loralena still. I love her so much it aches. Mem and Art gaze at me without seeing, and I want to reach out and tell them everything will be all right, but how can I say that when he is here even now? I can't promise a thing.

Ruin comes back with a roll of black plastic garbage bags and a stack of photograph albums. I recognize them; one from our wedding, one of the kids growing up, one of us in Candyland. "Yes, this is a very good idea," he says. "I should have thought of this myself. It will only make your suffering keener."

He shakes open the black bag and holds it open, then starts peeling photographs out of the album. He looks at each one for a moment, holds it out to me, then tears it to little pieces and drops it into the bag.

"Something for you to do," he says.

It takes hours. He goes through all the albums painstakingly, and when he's done with that he collects Mem's old rooster teddy and cuts it to chunks with a pair of kitchen scissors. He unloops the cotton stuffing within and makes a show of spooling it into the bag, like intestines. He cuts baby clothes to ribbons, smashes ornaments, plates, cups, cutlery and adds it all to the bag.

Every bit hurts. Every one is what I need, though I don't consciously know why.

At the end there are four full bags. He knots the top of each and tosses them to me. They land on the floor before me with a crunch and scrape.

"Now get out," says Ruin, "and if you ever come back again, well." He strolls over and lays his palm possessively on Loralena's cheek. "You know."

I pick up the bags and I leave.

It takes a month. I set up in Candyland atop the old wooden roller coaster. There's a platform there where Loralena and I sat, on the night I think Art was conceived.

I build the tower out of mortar dust ground from the park's old buildings, mixed with water from the sea to make a sticky paste. I blend the broken and torn fragments of photographs and letters into the paste, then daub it onto a frame of wood and nails I salvage from the roller coaster's support struts. It is like papier-mâché, one of the games I used to play with Art and Mem; building impossible figures from our imaginations.

The tower rises, rickety and creaking and filled with the memories of my life. When the regular pain comes from Mr. Ruin and my family, I focus it through this. The tower becomes a totem, amplifying my suffering and rewarding him more, as he'd hoped. I suffer more for it, am left gasping and sick since now I no longer drink, but there is a plan here somewhere even though I do not know what it is.

The tower rises a story high, then two stories, like a subglacic conning tower, and I plaster in the walls with mementos. At the top I fashion something like a periscope, jutting through the wooden ceiling. It is a haphazard affair, made of wooden planks with shards of warped mirror I found in the funhouse, but it works. I peer through it and see the cities of Calico spreading away like layers in the mind.

I scour the beaches around Candyland for days until I find enough rope, and a piece of wood suitable to serve for a wheel. It was once the top seal of a capstan, I think. I affix it at the head of my trembling tower atop the roller coaster, and look out over the world I have left behind.

The power of memories wells up around me, not only my own but also Lorelana's, Art's and Mem's. Their trails are everywhere here, the bonds hot and tight in this space where so much of our life together is now interred.

There is only one thing left to do.

In Calico it is easy to find Mei-An, with the power of the bonds behind me. She is a manager in an energy company now, specialized in ethical investment in renewable energy; trying to move the city on from hydrates.

I call her from a public node, and she comes to meet me in a coffee shop in the shadow of the wall. We sit in red plastic bucket seats and I look at her like a ghost from my past, and wonder about all the ways my life could have gone.

Now I come to her for help.

I look into her eyes. She is as beautiful as ever. She has grown into her implanted knowledge, building a proud and powerful woman out of the Skulk-touring youth she once was. In the background I can feel Mr. Ruin's curiosity as he watches us, and his confidence that there is nothing I can do. He is listening with me as I ask for the things I need.

"Please," I say, at the end.

Mei-An rests a hand on mine. She can see what has become of me. I wasn't much then, but I am nothing now. She could so easily say no, but she doesn't. "I'm so sorry. I tried to warn you."

I smile, and think back to a beeping text on a node from so long ago. She thinks that Don Zachary has brought me to this low ebb. Perhaps she thinks me his slave, doing his bidding all these years. She never knew Mr. Ruin. So I smile for her, to show that it is not so bad as that. Of course it is worse, but that's not her doing.

"It's all in the past," I say.

She leaves then comes back like a child sent out on a treasure hunt, bringing me good clothes, a node and enough money to pay for a hotel. These things are trifles for her, but impossible for me to attain on my own. I have no identity in this world anymore since Mr. Ruin took it, no name or money of my own.

I thank her, and she starts to cry. Perhaps she suspects, even as Mr. Ruin does, that this is some kind of last hurrah for me. That I am going to my death.

Perhaps. I kiss her hand, taste the scent of her unique skin I last tasted in another life and say goodbye.

I go to the hotel and wash, cleaning out the grime of a year. In the steamy heat of the shower I cut my hair and shave my scraggly beard, watching the filth swirl down the drain. I've done this before, one life shedding away for another. This is nothing new.

Mr. Ruin watches with amusement. I know for certain now; he thinks I will try to kill myself. He has prepared defenses against this; a line of control inside my own mind, implanted to prevent any such action. He will watch as I try, and be disappointed in me, and lick his lips as my punishment deepens.

In the evening I step out into the fresh Calico sea air, set to bring this farce to its end. I do not know what is going to happen, but I trust myself, that part of my mind which has saved me before; the child from a seven-toned womb that I once was, more vicious than anything I have become.

I stride up the steps toward the Wall train line, finally ready.

ME

L. SOLID ROCK

We race, and days pass us by. Corridor after corridor we run, metal turning to flesh as the many worms of the Lag hunt us down. In my HUD the blip of our flashing red dot penetrates deep into the Solid Core, running on faith that So calculated it right, that we're not even now speeding into the heart of a fractal off-shoot.

We shed memories like breadcrumbs at our backs. Piece by piece our memories of Ritry Goligh wear away as we shave them into slices and throw them out to keep the Lag from our heels. We forget every bit.

We grow weary. We snatch water and shock-jacks in what few moments we can, hunkered down in nodule-rooms that get darker and danker the further inward we go, with books of knowledge that get smaller and hazier. These are stories from a fragmented childhood now, of moments glimpsed by an infant mind and laid down in the unconscious record to build Ritry Goligh's unique mental architecture.

Ten or so rooms and twenty or more years of life later, there's nothing on the blood-mic but the distant, intermittet fuzz of So's ghostly voice, singing a lullaby.

We stop to catch our breath in a nodule very different to the rooms of the outer maze. The rusted metal walls are long-gone now, the signature RGs smoothed out into veiny seams of rock. Rather it's a murky, primordial cave; egg-shaped and marked with ridges, cracks and banded discolorations in the stone; a place before time. There are fossilized skeletons half-buried in the surface, barely visible in the gloom; the shapes of things that came before. It's hot and wet, and my wheezing breath condenses on the inner screen of my HUD.

I try to clear the visor but the vacuums are failing. I take off the HUD and run my finger around the suction cups, and something clicks loose. I hold it in my hand, a small chip of black plastic.

This equipment was not designed to last this long. None of us were. I look at the others, panting in the damp air. It smells of old things here, peat and a past long-buried. Doe's skin is whiter than the book I'm standing on, her cheeks sallow and drawn. Ray twitches in a half-sleep, haunted by nightmares of emptiness.

It's the same for me. I don't see Mr. Ruin or the Lag in the darkness behind my closed eyes; I see only the nothingness I've left behind.

Far trembles, now. I've tried holding him but it does nothing. The weals on his face and neck shine brightly like neon lights. Even when he's walking with us, he's suffering. Half the time we carry him because his legs won't hold him up. Sometimes when he tries to speak all that comes out are the same four tones. The panic in his eyes scares us all, shining through the defiance.

SAVE FAR

I think back on the mission folder's first directive, what feels like a lifetime ago. I am a different person now. I don't know what role Far is supposed to play, but I feel the importance of it. I love the boy like he was my own son, like he was me, and I know he will do all that he can to save us.

I set my broken HUD to the side and look down at the book beneath my feet. It is far thinner now and poorly stitched, in keeping with the degradation of our surroundings. There is no heavy leather cover, only a damp-mottled stretch of card atop cheap pulp paper. The pages within are blotted with dark scuffs; in places the handwritten text has been redacted with squiggling black lines.

Perhaps this is what was lost.

I read the few snatches of words for myself; they tell a splintered story of my infancy, or the infancy of Ritry Goligh. I am an expression of Ritry as he became, I think, only one version of the real man. The further we go in, the older the memories get, and these are all foreign to me.

We are close to the center now. A little further and we will be there with the first few cells of Ritry Goligh while the seven-tones of his artificial womb build him into existence. Further still, back beyond the arc of recollection to a place that is truly primal, we will hit the moment of conception, and perhaps answers will lie there. Perhaps there will be a bridge to something better, and a reason for all of this.

Abruptly, Far screams.

The noise is incredibly loud in the dark cavern, and without my HUD I cannot buffer it. The boy is sitting bolt upright and screaming, and at once I see why.

The Lag is in the room with us. We have become blind with exhaustion and it has snuck into our midst. Now its distended pink head is buried in Far's stomach. Blood spurts as it burrows deeper, and before I can even act Far's screams halt and his eyes roll up in his head.

I leap to the Lag and rip it out. It swallows my whole arm up to the elbow in turn, chipping deep divots into my sublavic suit. I rove with my fingers inside its gullet until I find the pieces of Far that it stole, then grip them hard.

"Kill it," I shout as Doe and Ray stir awake. Another slim Lag worm shoots across the space and hits Ray full in the HUD, knocking him flat onto his back inside the book.

The creature bites through my armor and up, chomping into my shoulder, and the pain is excruciating. I beat it with my free hand but to no avail. Doe is already astride it with a bayonet in her hand, sawing like So at the necks of the soldiers.

In three strokes she decapitates it; its jaws loosen and I pull my wounded arm out. Blood flows everywhere, whether from me or the ruins of Far's innards I don't know.

"Stabilize him, shock-jacks, transfuse, whatever you can," I shout as I lurch out of the way.

Doe goes to Far, unclipping tubes from her suit. Somewhere nearby Ray wrestles with his own Lag, his open hand stretching toward Doe. She places the bayonet smoothly in it as she kneels by Far, and Ray drives the blade through the monster's face, sealing its lips shut.

I activate sealant inside my suit and drop next to Far, already dizzy with blood loss. He is thrashing now with the impact of shock-jacks from Doe, his upper body jerking in time with her pulse. I hold out the fistful of viscera, glistening in our flickering suit lights. His heart is amongst the mulch, I think.

"It's going to be OK, Far," I say, though I am too terrified to believe it. Doe holds his head, his suit aorta linked in to her own, carrying her blood in only for most of it to spill out through his torn belly.

"Quickly, Me," she says.

I push my fist into the hole in Far's middle and deposit the organs that were stolen. They sit in the hole of his belly like food vomited from a mother chick's mouth, and I feel ashamed that this is all I can offer. I reach for the edges of his exo-suit to seal him up like La, but it seems the Lag must have ravaged it too thoroughly, as the edges don't match.

Doe is already stripping, pulling her suit off over her head. Beneath it she is all sinuous white flesh with a sweat-darkened shirt bound tightly across her chest.

"Get that off him," she says and I comply, fighting with Far's fading tremors to yank his arms out of the suit.

Ray drops beside me to help, covered in gore too, with ragged tears in his cheek where the beast caught him. Between us we tug Far's suit off then work to feed him into Doe's. It's large and we get his arms in easily then seal it over his bloody middle.

Ray breathes a sigh of relief. Doe closes the blood siphon off her throat and hands the tube to Ray, who plugs it in to his own.

"He'll be all right," says Ray, and though the words are hopeful I can't help but detect the desperation in his voice. Far has to be all right.

Doe slumps heavily, probably dizzy with the blood she's given, and points at the dead Lags. "Where did they come from?"

I rise and track the fleshy appendages. The lights on my suit have weakened so it's difficult to pick out the cracks where their bodies pass through the rock, but there are none. The conjunction is seamless; there is rock, then there is flesh.

"They didn't get in," I say. "They grew in."

Ray laughs, but there's no humor in it. "What the hell, Me?"

I prod the Lag's middle where it connects to the rock, but it doesn't peel away. It simply strains, and tight white sinew lines rise up along it like scars.

"It grew," I repeat. "This whole mind is turning against us."

"Out of solid rock?" Ray asks.

I don't have the strength to answer. None of us has strength to spare. Ray has Far's head against his chest now, rocking the boy unconsciously. Doe is sitting and breathing hard, her white skin glowing like an oxygen flare in the deepening dark.

Maybe this is where we all die.

There's so little of us left. I can barely breathe. I watch Far. Ray starts to turn pale and hands the blood siphon to me. I plug it into my neck; now the things I know will pass into Far, and whatever strength I have might keep him alive, but I have so little.

Ray's breath comes wetly. I should give commands but I don't know what to say. We can't move like this. We can't carry Far like this.

"You look nice," Ray says to Doe.

I'd laugh if I had the strength. She looks terrible. We all do. Her suit is off and she's rimed with sweat and oil and blood.

"Shut up," Doe manages.

"Pretty," Ray gulps. "I always thought so."

I look away. It would be awkward enough if they were just colleagues, but when they're tones in a shared chord, comprising component parts of a single gestalt entity, and they like each other, what can you say?

A long, breathless moment stretches out, then Doe speaks again.

"Fine," she says. "Let's do it."

I'm shocked. Ray is more shocked.

"It?" he asks, like he has no idea what she's talking about.

"Come over here."

I don't watch, but still I feel her long, willowy arm snaking out. Taking him by the hand. With what little strength they have, they stand, and lead each other into the shadows beyond the book.

I stop the flow of blood to Far before it kills me, and try not to listen as they fumble and groan in the dark. More intestinal worms could burst through the rock at any moment, but right now I don't care. This is the chord, my chord, and this is what Ray does best; he heals. Brings light to darkness. We all love each other, after all. You have to love yourself, to heal.

Their lovemaking is tender and urgent. She rises, he rises. It's a union, and through it I feel a new strength rising within me. Not a lot. Not a fire, but a seedling. A new memory all of our own; not one inherited from Ritry Goligh but something we made ourselves. In this place I consider it a wonder.

They finish together, sweaty, sticky and satisfied. I look to Far; his skin tone is clearer now. The artery in his neck pulses smooth and strong. Ray strides across the space behind me, pulling his armor back on.

"Come on, Me," he says, "can't sit around on the job." There's urgency in his tone, but there's also some of his cheeky irreverence, returned. I'm glad to hear it. "The Lag's right by your head."

I turn, and see the rock beside me distending. I jerk away as the tendril of a Lag worm grows a speck of flesh at a time, exuding out of the rock. Ray punches it flat.

Our reprieve is over. It's time to finish this mission. Ray fits Far in his holster, Doe kicks out the door and we run back out into the tunnels. Heads ducked, we sprint fast and cramped through dark and dripping caves, on pathways bored through solid stone as though by giant insects, skirting stalagmites and stalactites with the glow of new love encircling us and our pulsing red dot inching ever closer to the heart of the Solid Core.

M. ARTIFICIAL WOMB

The tunnels change as we cross some unseen line into the Solid Core's inner sanctum, becoming metal-framed corridors embossed with the RG initials.

Ritry Goligh.

As we run, stamping drumrolls with our footfalls, we speak of this man who was our creator and embodies us in ways we cannot understand.

"We're all aspects of him," Ray says as we pass down a dark, narrow hall. There are few turnings now; the maze has simplified to a single path, and I haven't seen the Lag for hours, but that hasn't stopped the waking visions.

They come hardest for Far. He naps in Ray's side-holster and screams in his sleep. His stomach seems to have repaired itself, but I fear his mind is fatefully damaged. Those few seconds with his heart lost to the Lag have changed him.

Ray goes on. "Far is Ritry as a boy. I'm the changes all his friends made in him; Ferrily and Tigrates, Carrolla. Doe is what Ven left; cold and hard and in control."

"I can imagine captaining a subglacic," Doe says. The blood-mic sputters often now, so we run with our HUDs up most of the time, only pulling them down to periodically listen to the distant sighing of So's lullabies, somewhere in a world far gone. "I think I'd be good at it."

She runs alongside Ray when the way is wide enough, which is touching. I remember enough to know Ven hated Tigrates and Ferrily.

"So what am I?" I ask.

"You're some kind of amalgam," Doe says. "The man evolved."

"And So?" I ask. "The others."

Ray answers. "So is Loralena, Me."

There is quiet but for the clanging of our feet.

"I think the gravity is getting heavier here," I say.

"Did you hear what Ray said?" Doe asks.

I look back at them both. "I heard you," I say. "I know."

So, who still isn't dead, who hangs on behind singing us forward. So is Loralena.

I blink and rub my eyes.

"It is getting heavier," Doe says. "It's hard to even lift my arms."

We run on. Now there are shapes carved into the walls, like ancient Egyptian gods. Here is a face I should recognize, but do not. There are figures scampering in the darkness.

"A mother," Ray mutters to himself, barely captured on blood-mic. "A father?"

We come upon an open archway to the side, cut directly into the wall. There has been nothing like it so far, and before I can stop him Ray runs in.

"Wait," I say, but Doe follows, and I follow her.

It is a dark cave, bar the glow coming from a tubular glass tank in the middle, topped with complex metal machinery. The tank is filled with pale green fluid, with a thick cable hanging down inside and inserted into the middle of a half-formed baby, like a mechanical umbilical cord.

The baby is pink, floating in the liquid, and he is looking back at us with tiny gray eyes.

"Young Ritry," says Far.

He waits behind us in the arch. I didn't notice him dismounting from the side-holster. He hasn't spoken for what feels like days, and the sound startles me.

"Come in, Far," Ray says.

"No," says Far, "I can't let him see me."

"Why not?"

Far doesn't answer. He makes no further move toward us, so we turn back to the forming baby in the tank. Doe presses her face close to the glass with tears running down her cheeks. I have never seen Doe cry.

"I'm sorry," she whispers to the little floating figure. "I'm so sorry."

I can hear the seven tones of the artificial womb in the air now, playing in unison like a chord. There is no pulse to it, no familiar thump-thump, only an endless blend of notes like a funeral dirge for lost family, but it is not mournful. Here, like this, it is comforting. It makes me feel safe and at home.

Then I hear a shuffle. There is something lurking in the darkness. I cannot resolve it, a shape scarcely more than a shadow, but the very notion of it terrifies me. Even here in this sacred place he exists.

"Mr. Ruin," Far says.

I stop breathing. I watch this dark figure as he slinks in the shadows. Even before we were born, he was watching.

"He's not really here," Doe says, wiping away the tears, but her voice is uncertain, as though she's trying to convince herself. "It's just a memory."

Slowly the dark figure circles his way closer to the glass, seeming to bring the darkness with him. We shuffle to make way. All I can see of his face is the glint of white teeth. He presses close to the machine womb's glass, then taps on it with his finger like a child at an aquarium, hankering for the attention of the fish.

Little Ritry Goligh turns to face him. His half-formed gray eyes blink. Stalked before he was even born.

"I'm going to kill this fucker," says Doe.

Ray is shaking with rage beside me. I feel it too, welling up from everything I am, but these are shadows only. There is no use in smashing the past. It's what's happening right now that matters most; it's Ritry Goligh's present that we can change.

I lay a hand on both of their shoulders and lead them out. "We will kill him," I promise. "I don't know how, but I swear it."

Far gives me a long look as we leave. I think for a moment I glimpse some resolve hidden within him, some hint of deeper thoughts turning far below, but then it is gone and he is back to being just a weary, brutalized boy. He reaches for my hand and I take it. We run on together, while Ray and Doe clutch each other and beat their way down the hall.

"I'm sorry," says Far as we run.

"For what?" I ask.

"For what's coming."

I don't press it. I wonder, am I the captain of the chord now, or is Far?

Then we reach the end.

Our red dot flashes up against the heart of So's map in my HUD; the center of the Solid Core. We have reached our destination. Before us stands a huge blast door made of corroded black metal, riveted with rusted bolts like the exterior of the Solid Core. I run my gloved fingers over it, feeling the imperfections. This thing is ancient.

There is no handle and no hinge. We pry at its seams and Ray shoulders it firmly, but it doesn't budge. I look at Doe and she nods.

"Go back, Far," I tell the boy. He nods, so pale. His weals burn bright in the blackness, but he looks at me with trust and understanding in his eyes. We are a chord, and we will do this together.

Doe prepares the dregs of our candlebomb, melting it into place around the frame of the corroded door. I smell ozone and scorched plastic. Wax dribbles over her fingers and down her suit.

"Careful," Ray breathes in her ear, "don't ignite it prematurely."

She whispers something about this not being her first rodeo. They work together to construct the lines of the bomb aligned to the cracks in the door while I spool out the remaining fuse.

We're almost there.

RITRY GOLIGH

18. BRINK

The train roars into the station with a percussive wind, thunderously loud, and people pour out. They flow either side of me like molten rock, so hot I can feel the energy burning off them.

Things are changing for me now. Already I see things differently. People are memories and the Lag at once. They are all the same, and none of them are like me.

I fold into the carriage. A man with a jaw like a toad glares at me. I look out of the glass as the doors hiss shut and some of the groaning engine sound is cocooned away. The train gets underway, the lights of Calico Central station rush by, and then there is darkness. In the black of the glass I study my reflection.

Do I look different now? It's hard to know. I wonder at the calm I'm feeling inside, and I glance over the faces of the other commuters around me. They're tapping on nodes, staring vacantly up at the rack-ads, picking at their cuticles; all living their lives, going from place to place, all with their little bits of complexity, wonder and misery.

I could pull them apart at the seams. I could become just like Mr. Ruin if I wanted, crack them open like eggs and eat. But I'm not like Mr. Ruin and I never was.

I'm me.

My face looks different in the glass. Thinner and older. It is a year since I cared to see a mirror.

The train hisses into another station and I am vomited out by the press of bodies. Already my brand new suit clings to my skin. I feel the humidity soaking in like alcohol, trying to fog my mind. I move through the press. Somebody strikes me in the shoulder as he goes by, and I feel his scorn. He is a cruel and angry man, another bully with a briefcase.

I have time enough for this. I catch up to him through the flow and step around to face him. He's taller than me, strong as I once was, with sandy hair that slides either side of his face. He seems momentarily surprised, then he recognizes me and the scorn comes back.

"Having a bad day?" I ask, and jam my new node into his crotch. He gasps and doubles over. This is not a Skulk and I am not beyond the law, but I don't care. I can't be stopped now. I grab the back of his head and for a moment imagine ramming the node into his unprotected face five times, cracking his jaw, knocking three teeth loose, maybe imploding an eyeball. It's the kind of thing I might once have done. Far off, Mr. Ruin thrills at the prospect.

Instead I push the node up into his throat and squeeze his windpipe. He's about to start struggling but as the edge of the metal digs into his throat his body goes slack. He thinks I have a knife. I lean in and whisper in his ear.

"I should kill you. What do people like you bring to the world? What's the point of you? We'd all be better off with you buried in the fucking dirt."

These are barely even words meant for him; I know it as I say them. But this is the most restrained I can be.

I feel his mind recoil. He is full of fear now, the scorn gone. I feel his miserable, small Soul, and the cruelty he indulges in when he can. He is a sadist like Mr. Ruin, and I hate nothing more than sadists now.

I Lag him. Perhaps I am the cruel one, to do this. I take every bit of pleasure he ever gained from cruelty, and leave only the sour guilt that remained afterward. He is clay in my hands and I am changing things now, finally.

On his knees he begins to sob, as the unmitigated weight of all he has done crumples him. He has become a lost man, as I have been for so long. Perhaps it will be a new start.

I leave him there and return to the train. I feel Mr. Ruin's distant delight. He thinks I am becoming more like him; beginning to savor the pain of others as a source of power.

The train rises up through the tsunami wall to the open top, where people alight for shopping and sightseeing over the Arctic Ocean. The train's rhythm steadies out. Clack clack, clack clack, clack clack we go, along this string of walled cities that make up the isthmus; from Calico Central to Tenbridge Wulls, from Tenbridge Wulls to Saunderston, all the way to the end. There we descend gradually as the wall ramps down to the natural coast. I get off the express and wait at a dim station for the tram to the little town of Brink, and Candyland.

I ride the tram alone. These rails are old, built over two hundred years ago, once atop a ridge and now skirting a coast. Now my reflection in the glass is spiked by the light of shored hydrate tankers, unloading fuel at the proto-Calico wall pumps. On the horizon there's a single bright point of light wrapped with fuzzy old bonds of violence. This is one of the Arctic rigs we fought so hard for, sucking hydrates out of the ancient ocean bed, once covered by ice. Now they stand across the whole of the North, sucking the last rotting succor out of the bodies of dead dinosaurs buried far below.

We are everywhere now. We have consumed everything. There are no more dark spots on the map but the ones we've left behind.

It's nearly midnight by the time I reach the final station, Brink. The night porter walks by holding his ticket ticker.

"Here for the Mass lights?" he asks.

I shake my head. He points out the window and I see colored fairy lights dancing in long lines over the small station outbuildings and around the curved spine of the single bench. I didn't notice them before.

"No," I say, getting to my feet, "I'm visiting friends."

He gives me an odd look, but takes the ticket from my hand and punches a hole through it.

"You best hurry then," he says, "they'll be closing down the line soon." He carries on to the carriage end.

The doors open and I leave the tram behind.

I walk through the little town of Brink past shuttered windows and doors. The air smells of hot tar and brown sugar. I catch tinny music leaking from a second floor apartment, a bar of some sort, with faint voices livening up the night. Once that was my life too.

Candyland is waiting for me, this one dark patch at the map's edge, where I will make my final stand. Now the saccharine air mixes with the scent of seeping vegetation. Walking across the empty parking lot, old memories bubble up. We came here together and held hands. The park was already dead but still we came to play. Here I held Art's hand. Here I kissed Loralena. Here I once pulled up in Don Zachary's speedboat.

A different life.

It grows very dark at the entrance, and barbed wire rustles in my hair as I clamber through the rusted turnstile. Boulder-like shapes lie in the shadows; under my fingers the heat of the sun still buzzes within their lifeless frames. They are toppled fishing boats, dropped here by a tsunami long ago. Down the main promenade there is jungle to either side. I still smell the refining sugar, but it is fading, replaced by hints of popcorn, the acrid burn of fireworks exploding overhead and the flowery shampoo smell of Mem's hair as she pulls me down to whisper in my ear:

"This is wonderful, Daddy."

The memory of a memory. Only I saw this place alive.

I walk up the steep wooden roller coaster tracks to the apex of the dive, rising far above the land below. Here is my tower, standing as tall as the Calico wall and built with everything I have left. I enter and begin the slow ascent up the circling staircase, stroking the curved wall with the backs of my fingers. The surface is rough and granular, made out of memory. It is a cast of my life and the life of my family, and the reason my mind is so clear, because I'm going to take it all back.

My skin tingles in the charged air. I have known this pain for so long.

I arrive at the top and look out on the park and the world. Overhead old satellites circle through the stars. Across the park lie the twin cities I've forsaken, both Calico and the shadow sprawl of proto-Calico hugging the wall. This is all we have left.

The wheel before me is as large as the wheel on a subglacic, connected to vents and flues throughout the tower. Everything is perfectly balanced and I am ready, just as I always was as a marine in the Arctic War, ready to fight for my right to exist. I lay my hands on the smooth handles and allow myself a brief moment to repeat a promise I made to Mr. Ruin all those years ago.

To drown him in his own mind.

Everything is to play for now.

I lift the wheel and it clicks to engage. I feel the wind about me rush to fill the ventricles in the Tower, like blood through a pumping heart. The cement beneath my feet vibrates. I turn the wheel, and the thumping begins.

I feel the wave rise on a tide of the bonds.

It's beginning.

I jack in.

Down into my own mind I plunge, buoyed by the strength of the tower. Layers of thought pummel me like bubbles until I lose all sense of my body and the world around me, jacking deeper until my own Molten Core is a red glow ahead.

I hit the blazing magma hard, too fast for Mr. Ruin to stop me, and consciousness falls away like protective brick cladding. Everything I am splits into the seven constituent tones of my mind's architecture, each one burning into existence in forging pods within the sublavic ship.

Doe, Ray, Me, Far, So, La, Ti.

They rouse and for an instant some sense of me is still with them, writing the mission folder they will soon read, painting the map they will need across the captain's chest, because for a brief moment only I see it all. I have glimpsed what violence lies ahead; I understand what is required to truly break free of Mr. Ruin's desecrating touch. It is terrifying and beautiful and beyond my comprehension.

Then it is gone, as my last sense of self is swept away in the forging and I come to in one mind only, Me, coughing up treacle-black smoke in the rusted corridors of the sublavic, with the pod-forge flaming me to life and the screw failing and the air filled with the stink of burning brick.

ME

N. THE BRIDGE

Huddled by the blast-door we talk in low fast whispers as Doe trims the wicks of the candle-bomb, aligning the gamma-clamp to corrosion marks in the huge black blast-door. Ray is talking into his blood-mic to So back at the outer orbit, his piercing green eyes on me.

"Anything you can give us, So, on what's on the other side, anything at all."

As ever, no answer comes. I flip up the chronometer function on my HUD. Has it already been a week in this maze?

Far calls us to hurry from the end of the corridor. His trembling shadow casts a long way down in the orange oxyfer lights, and I gesture to him to be calm. I try to project my soothing vibes out to him, but it's hard when there's sweat beading down my face and pooling in the dead vacuum cups gathered under my eyes. I nod to Ray, who was always better at morale, and he smiles to Far, which helps.

"T-minus three," says Doe, wiping her greasy hands on her black double-breasted flak jacket. I try to blink the panic-sweat out of my eyes but it won't dissipate. The HUD vacuums stopped working days ago. Everything here reeks of sweat.

Ray claps a hand on my shoulder. I look through his visor and see his big grin and bright white teeth inset with loop piercings like some ridiculous mesh of braces.

"You crying, Me?" he asks.

"It's the vacuums," I say. "They don't work."

He chuckles like I'm telling a lie.

"T-minus two," says Doe, and turns to face me. Her white albino face stares like a ghost. Her fingers are covered in candlewax. "Nearly there," she says.

"What's the problem?"

She points at the fuse; it's already blackened, as though the spark wouldn't take.

"This length is a dud," she says. "Everything's failing."

"So fire it remotely," says Ray, his sharp green gaze meeting Doe's pink irises.

She shakes her head. "Transmitters are broken, and I don't have enough fuse left to get us out of range. We used most of it on the Deathgate."

A beat passes.

Down at the end of the corridor Far whimpers something. He's been seeing monsters for hours; I expect he's seeing one now. I've been seeing them too, ever since I pulled one out of his guts. They come big and small, they come with jaws and suckers and they devour us all

Ray nudges me and I jerk back to the present.

"Use my arm as fuse," he says. "The skin will conduct." He doesn't need to think about it. This is who he is; anything for the team. It doesn't make much sense to me, but what does in this place?

Doe looks at me and I look at her.

"Maybe just a few fingers," she says. "If I lay them end to end. They might just put us around the corner."

Ray holds up his left hand, grabs Doe's trimming tool from her waxy grip, and chops off his little finger.

It drops to lie amongst the floor's printed RG initials, like some kind of meaningful augur. Blood pools around it. Doe gazes at Ray and I know what she's thinking. One more. Ray lifts the clippers but before he can do it I've raised my own hand.

"You do it," I say, holding my hand out to him. He grins.

"I thought you'd ever ask." He clamps the fuse-trimmer around the base of my little finger and snips it off. The digit drops to lie neatly next to his, and I wonder briefly what that could possibly mean; like tea leaves telling our fortune. Blood pours out but I pinch the suit sealed over the wound.

Doe gathers up the fingers and aligns them with the existing fuse.

"Let's hope this is the last door," says Ray.

I give a token dry laugh, then Doe motions us to get back. "Lead time of fifteen seconds, then it'll blow."

"Far, we're coming," I call to the kid, "T-minus ten around the corner."

He shuffles out of sight.

Ray claps a hand on my shoulder. "It's been an honor," he says.

"The honor's mine," I reply, and look to Doe as well. "To serve with you both."

She grunts, then sparks the fuse. It fizzes to life and we sprint away together, the metal floor clanging beneath our feet. Around the corner we hunker down to join Far where he's huddled in a ball, squeezing our eyes tight shut and cupping our ears until-

BOOM

I catch the B- of it before the sound becomes too loud to even hear. Light flares around us then I'm up and charging into the aftermath of the blast. The floor is melting with the heat, smoke and vaporized metal streams off my HUD and I speed through the ruin of the door barely seeing a thing until I burst into -

A room that is not a room, in a space that is not a space, in the midst of the thing we've come all this way to find.

The center of the Solid Core.

I barely keep to my feet. Ahead of us lies a universe. It spreads out into blackness for distances I can't fathom, filled with a trillion stars spread around two massive red suns at the center. I waver in awe. It is everything and nothing at once, a secret dimension lying above or below reality, and before its splendor I feel myself begin to drift.

I am Me, captain of the ship, but I am also Doe, and Ray, and Far and So and La and Ti, and Ritry Goligh, and Ven and Ferrily and Tigrates and Heclan and Carrolla and my biological mother and father who I never met and Mr. Ruin too, and Loralena and Mem and Art all at once like we're all individual cells building into one vast fetus floating in the universe's machine womb.

"Ritry Goligh," says Ray by my side, and it is my mouth and my voice that breathe the words, and my ears that hear them, and my mind that made them.

All these stars are Souls, I realize, perhaps all the Souls alive and all that ever lived. If I squint I can seen the countless silvery lines of bonds linking them together and shining like comet trails across the black. The air is so thick with connection it should be solid: friendships, relationships, family ties, chance encounters, inspirations, memories, stories all linking people to people to people in an indescribably complex web.

"Sweet Goligh," Doe murmurs, now weeping openly. Her hands hang slack; there is nothing to fight here. We are at once standing in space, and lying on the ceiling, and swirling at light speed forward and backward and spaghettified by the black hole mass of it all tat the same time. La and Ti are with us now, singing, and So too; we are all here again.

I think I understand something that Far always knew, that all good things require sacrifice, and this is the sacrifice we have come to make.

I turn to Far and he smiles at me. In this place all his weals are gone and he is smiling. He is the master of our seven-toned Soul, I see that now, and its ultimate protector. I always thought I was the one bringing him here, but I see now that he was the one bringing us.

"And I'll bring you back," he says to me, in my own voice, "I swear it."

Then he plunges his musket bayonet into Ray's chest. Ray bursts in a shower of fizzing white energy. Doe nods with understanding as he plunges the blade into her next, releasing more force that crackles around us both.

I spread my arms like an icon from the godship temple and smile at this child of mine, this part of me both innocent and utterly vicious at once.

ONE OF YOUR CHORD WILL KILL YOU ALL.

We are the sacrifice. We are the bonds that will fuel him on.

"Thank you," I say, and he spears the bayonet through the center of the maze written across my chest and into my heart, and I am gone, my matter converted to energy with all the fissile strength of a hydrogen bomb.

O. FAR

The boy Far stood in the center of consciousness and looked out over the aether. He'd never come here before, though he'd come close once, driven by the tortures of his parents. Their lessons had taught him so much: how to breathe molten lava, how to tame the Lag, how to build a trap out of scar tissue powerful enough to smother them all.

He saw the dizzying array of bonds arcing outward. They were inconceivably complex, linking a trillion souls across the aether into a single pulsing fire. He reached for one in particular; a star that shone brighter than the others, that had haunted him since before he was born, and he plucked at it.

Mr. Ruin stood in an apartment in Calico Reach with his blades in his hands, bringing them down upon Loralena, Art and Mem. Seconds ago Ritry Goligh had initiated a jack into his own Molten Core, and now the punishment was due. Excitement sparked through him as the blades swept down; an appetizer only, to be followed by the final extinction of Ritry Goligh himself.

Then something happened.

He couldn't see it as Far came in like an assassin from the aether, through an inner bridge he didn't know existed. He didn't understand what was happening when all his memories of Ritry's family were abruptly Lagged away, though he felt the sting. It burned like a cauterized stump in his mind, so he no longer knew why he was standing over this terrified woman and these children with his knives in his hands. At once they were meaningless to him.

All that remained was a name, and Far injected that name like an engram deep into Mr. Ruin's Soul, etching blazing letters five-feet high onto the rusted metal of his Solid Core.

Ritry Goligh.

Instantly it enraged and consumed him, making Ritry Goligh an indelible part of his mental architecture in a way he'd never been before. Now Ruin would hunt with an all-consuming ferocity until he found and broke his prey, and this time there would be no long drawn-out tortures and no search for the Solid Core. There would only be death.

Then Far was yanked backward through the aetheric universe, his power spent, glimpsing only briefly the glory of the twin red suns burning and revolving, and a distant purple star spitting out electric pulses, and a universal aether made up of endless connections that linked every Soul to each other in a glorius whole. Howling forces dragged him back and flung him out through the ruptured blast door.

He leaned in to the momentum, flying so hard he punched a hole clear out of the fractal maze and past poor disembodied So surrounded by the headless corpses of Ruin's Napoleonic guards. He shot out of the Solid Core through the Deathgate and hit the Molten Core below with a joy he hadn't felt in years. This was his home, the prison he'd been forged within, and into it he breathed out the seven primal tones of his own Soul's architecture: Doe, Ray, Me, Far, So, La, Ti, ringing them out through the lava.

Like a fetus inflating within an artificial womb, the Bathyscaphe built itself from memory around him, and the six marines that made up the rest of his chord came with it; Me at the bridge and Doe by his side, Ray manning the trim tanks, So and La on the coolant stacks and Ti down at the engine screw driving them, driving them, driving them forth.

All together again.

RITRY GOLIGH

19. TOGETHER

The world spits me out complete, Ritry Goligh once more, and I sag to the floor of my memory tower shaking as the immense weight of terror lifts for the first time in a year.

They are safe.

It is all that matters. The relief is impossibly sweet. I can feel Mr. Ruin coming for me but I don't care. My family's long year of torture and loss has finally come to an end, and they are safe.

I laugh and cry at the same time, standing at the tower top with my hands on the wheel still, like Me in the conning tower of his Bathyscaphe. I remember all that my chord did for me: the noble sacrifice of Ti to get us out of the Molten Core, La fighting Ruin's soldiers to the death, So remaining behind as our anchor, Doe, Ray and Me giving their lives at the end to fuel Far's final transgression.

Crossing the last door into the heart of the Solid Core. I remember the wonders I saw and they fill me still. Stars rush inside me like Souls, and I feel them all spread across the world. So many people and so much hope.

Now Ruin is coming, and I am ready. At last I understand Far's plan, and what this tower I have built truly is.

I descend the spiral stairs to the roller coaster's wooden rails, and drop to my knees in the shadowy middle. Here the air is split by bars of morning light that shine through the holes in the tower, opened when I turned the wheel above.

The chord begin to slip from my grasp as I shuffle back into the darkness. Just moments ago I held them within the palm of my hand, but now the details are fading. I say a silent thanks as they dwindle away, and the wounds in my mind begin to heal over with fresh scar tissue.

All memories are scars.

I kneel in the dust of my tower, in the sun-shafted darkness, and wait for Mr. Ruin. I feel him out there like a shark in the deep. He doesn't know about my family anymore. He never understood the power of devotion, because he has never loved a thing more than himself. The family he helped me to find have made me strong in ways he will never understand.

I rub my eyes. How long did I jack for, and what did I see? Maybe seconds only, though it felt like days. There are only glimpses of the invasion left now, my chord of marines in a dark space fighting soldiers and the wormy Lag with cannon and bayonets.

I am dizzy and exhausted, and I wait.

I rouse from a fugue with Mr. Ruin standing in the archway to the tower. It is early afternoon, judging by the gray light filtering through the slits and haloing him from behind. The inside of the tower is murky, filled with dust and memory.

He watches me as I blink to full consciousness, as I remember who and where I am; not the captain of a chord racing into the depths, but a man in a tower made of ruin. He's wearing his gray shark suit, and he looks no older than the day I first saw him in the ruined arena. I can feel the blinding fury I wrote into him, raging now within his steely shell.

"Not bad," he says, penning the rage in. His teeth shine in the deepening dark. "It's the first time since Napoleon that anyone fought this hard. I have to respect that."

I laugh, a shallow barking sound. There is the dust of pounded memories in my throat. He doesn't know what he's doing here. He doesn't know what I've done.

"You don't respect me. You didn't respect Napoleon. You're empty inside."

He gives a light shrug. This doesn't touch him. "I honor Napoleon, as I will honor you, Ritry." He takes a step into the darkness, savoring the moment. "I admit, I never expected him to escape Elba a second time, just as I did not expect this from you. He was a rascal, really. Such charisma. You don't remind me of him in that regard."

I shuffle further backward in the dark. "You've come for more than insults."

He grins, feigning confidence, but there's uncertainty there too. "You're right. You did something to me, Ritry, didn't you?" He wags his cane. "But what? You took something from me, and I didn't know what at first, or how." He pauses, taking another step in. "But I do now."

I glare up at him, feeling the fear he wants me to feel, because I am afraid. He is no fool. He is and always was a killer, and he is still stronger than me.

"It explains all this," he goes on, gesturing at the tower around us. "This contraption. Is it a lens, Ritry? You focused your considerable skill. You jacked the Molten Core against my explicit direction." The cane wags admonishingly, another step in. "You killed the guards I left there and you dared to enter the Solid Core. You know that's what I wanted." Now his eyes gleam with excitement. He can barely breathe with anticipation. "You breached the aetheric bridge, didn't you? I always knew you could." JHis expression sours. "Then you used it to steal something from me. What did you take, you clever little boy? You clever little shit."

I gaze back, defying him. It only makes him angrier, bringing the rage to the surface and boiling off him like lava in the Molten Core. I need him angry and blind.

"What did you take, Ritry?" He stamps closer, shaking the tower on its rail-top frame. "What have you stolen from me?"

"It wasn't yours," I say. "It never was."

His eyes flare wide, and I think for a moment that I have pushed too far and he will simply Lag me lying here, in the ruins of the ruin of my life. But he is too curious for that, too hungry to understand. With visible effort he calms himself and takes another step into the gloom, so close now he could touch the central tower column.

"You see the pins you have in me, Ritry? Tweak them a little in and I explode. But perhaps that is what you want? A quick ending. I won't grant it." He's calmer now, the shark tucked away deep in his belly, the smooth gray veneer back. "It's what Napoleon begged for in the end, as I screwed the spirit out of his beloved Josephine, while he could only languish on his shitty island just like you in this place. I had to send a message, you see. The utter depths of his defeat were delicious. But where's your Josephine now, Ritry? I could swear I had her, but she's gone. Is that what you took?"

I don't say anything. I feel the rough timber boards beneath my knees. A little further only.

"You'll never have them again," I say.

His grin widens. "A family, perhaps. And how will you stop me? I'll say it again, I'm impressed, but to what end? You've bought a few hours for yourself. Now it's really about professional respect. You don't make a snake cough up its dinner then expect it to be friendly. You don't steal flies from the web and expect forgiveness."

"I thought you were a shark."

He chuckles. "You'll beg again, don't worry. I know how to make it happen." He reaches into his jacket pocket and pulls out a glistening silver and glass cylinder. It is a Soul Jacker's syringe with a wickedly long needle, long enough to press through the eye socket and directly into the brain. Even in the dim light I can see the heavy silver liquid in the chamber, as certain as a bullet.

It is liquid memory, but a dose a thousand times larger than I've ever dealt. It could be language, skill, memory; it doesn't matter anymore since the contents must have been mixing for hours. It is a cocktail that will flood my mind in an instant, surging past the scarification maze around my Solid Core to sweep my Soul away like a tsunami.

I shuffle backward until I'm up against the rough plaster wall, sweating cold and hard. I hadn't expected this, and he luxuriates in it. "Oh, Ritry," he says. "You were never really ready for me. What shark retreats? They would stop breathing and die. For those like you and me, there is only forward." He takes the next step closer, and I brace myself into a small gap in the tower's metal scaffold.

He holds the syringe out to the side so it catches the last of the dying light. "This is from your old office, by the way. I had to raid all the new Jacker's supplies to get enough. Didn't you say this to me, that you'd drown me in my own mind?" He cocks his head thoughtfully. "I don't think it will be fast. It certainly won't be pleasant, because you'll still be in there, won't you? How far can you retreat before the rising waters get you? You'll have to give up yourself one piece at a time, just like you did in the War, until it's all gone. Can you imagine what that would be like? You'll do it yourself, Ritry, and I will sit here and watch."

The old arrogance is back. He takes the final step, then squats on his haunches to better see me.

"Unless."

He squeezes the syringe, so a tiny drip of thick silver liquid twinkles at the tip. His voice drops low and rough. "Unless you teach me how to jack the bridge. That would be worth something. A change of execution, maybe a little mercy, perhaps even a partnership of some kind, in time, if you're a good boy and know your place. Can you imagine the possibilities, Ritry?" He looks at me with the wonder back in his eyes. "I could Lag them all at once; I would never go hungry again. I would be King and you will be my jester, trusted member of my court. Come, Ritry, it's far more than Napoleon got."

He stares at me and I stare back. I can feel how eager he is now, how hungry, and I know that it will never end. Like a shark he will continue until everything is under his thumb, until everyone is reduced to begging on their knees. I would rather feed myself to the Lag than leave him alive in this world.

"Never," I say."

"Very well," he says, then lunges forth with both the syringe and his mind at the same time.

It is almost enough. His mind freezes me, the syringe flashes toward my eye, but there's enough of Far in me left to do what I have to.

I yank a lever in the scaffold and something gives.

The syringe bursts through the corner of my eye and penetrates down along the optic nerve. I feel Ruin's wild abandon as he starts to depress the punger, pumping millions of points of data into my mind.

Then the tower collapses.

It comes with a roar as so much brick and wood comes loose from its moorings. The rails below us tremble as the walls, stairs, floors and ceiling of my scar-tissue tower come crashing down like a tsunami wave, crushing Mr. Ruin and hammering off my protective metal cage at the edge like the Lag pounding at the door.

Control of my body returns as Mr. Ruin jerks into unconsciousness, buried beneath a heap of masonry, and I pluck at the syringe in my eye. It slides out with a kissing sound and I blink out the silvery excess, then close my eyes to fend off the first tsunami of information.

As the last chunks of my tower patter off the rubble pile I jack into the outer depths of my own Molten Core and summon the Lag. It is my beast now, a dog I can direct at will, and I set it upon the surging flood of data threatening to extinguish my Soul. It opens its many mouths to eat.

Hours pass while the world turns with me and Mr. Ruin at the center. The Lag works quickly and efficiently and I feed it like a trusted pet, leashed and collared. Every bit of nonsense knowledge cut away makes me stronger as the bonds break and convert to energy.

At the same time Mr. Ruin is dying. He can barely breathe and his blood is leaking out. He reaches out to me through the rubble and dust, but I pat his hand away. He reaches out with his mind but his strength is gone.

Soon the few drops of silver liquid he squeezed into me have been digested. I open my eyes in the darkness, to find his face lit by a few faint cracks of moonlight shining in through chinks in the rubble.

"A trap," he whispers.

He is staring at me with dark blood on his lips, caked with dust and froth. He tries to laugh and I feel his pain.

"Spider," he croaks. "Not shark. You did well, Ritry. I'm proud of you."

I stare at him through the dust, and scoop up the syringe. "You don't get to talk to me anymore," I say. "You don't get to say anything."

He sees the syringe and his eyes go wide. Fear blooms in him, and his body relinquishes control of his bladder, dripping piss down through the roller coaster timbers.

"You can't have them," he whispers in a hoarse cry, "they're mine!"

He's too weak to resist. He goes cold with rage and terror as I press the needle into his eye socket, then starts to laugh as I depress the plunger.

"You think you're free?" he whispers feverishly. "You think they didn't feel it too, when you broke through the bridge? They all know you now, Ritry!"

I lean closer, one hand on his hot and dusty head and one holding the syringe, and look into his gray predator eye.

"You don't know me at all," I say, and drive the plunger home. A million billion points of data swarm into his mind. His dark eyes widen and he mouths meaningless sounds as his brain is flushed clean.

CODA

I ride the Wall line back to the city. It is nearly dawn, and in the still dark glass of the train window I see myself reflected.

Ritry Goligh. This is who I am. A man made of a seven-toned chord. An Arctic marine, a Soul Jacker to the Skulks and to Calico, now husband, father and survivor.

I brush the dust on my suit away. I pull out the node from Mei-An and key in a number I memorized long ago. It rings and I feel them out there still, my family, still trapped in the old nightmare and waiting for me to come home.

They have been waiting for such a long time.

Now I'm coming. The node rings and I reach out to their bonds through the air. The node rings, and the first glimmer of the morning sun rises up over the tsunami wall, eclipsing my reflection and the tears in my eyes with glowing orange light.

I'm finally going home.

AUTHOR'S NOTE

Soul Jacker was one of the first books I wrote, after The Saint's Rise. It began life titled Mr. Ruins and was deeply inspired by my life in Japan. Ritry is a kind of glorified teacher, just as I was a teacher in Tokyo. He explored ruins and found a new strength within them, much as I did.

The rest comes from the imagination. From the aether, if you will - snatched down off the bonds. I wrote it a year before I left Japan to come live in London, UK, in 2014. I poured everything I had into it, using all my knowledge from my degree in Psychology, harnessing the complex ideas and puzzlebox narrative style I'd loved in movies like The Matrix and Inception.

I published it with great excitement, but it didn't catch on. In later years I learned some of the reasons: maybe the cover was wrong, the genre was wrong, the text itself was difficult. I had new covers made. I worked on the text to make it less dense.

Now I've gone the whole way with a major rewrite. The genre is plainly cyberpunk, and this is reflected in the new title and cover. The text and ideas are as clear and exciting as I know how to make them. The puzzlebox narrative structure of interweaving chapters remains, but it conjoins in a much smoother way than before. What we have here is Ritry and the chord's story; as clear and clean as it has ever been. It's taken five years but I think I'm there. I hope you've enjoyed it.

If you have, please consider reviewing it on your favored shop site - reviews are huge for me, not only in guiding how I write but also in helping other readers make their reading decisions. You can also get a free copy of The Last by joining my newsletter –

www.michaeljohngrist.com/newsletter-sign-up

In acknowledgement, I want to thank Rob Nugen for offering great suggestions, my Dad for encouragement, Matt Finn and many others for sharing great insights on how to streamline and improve the book, and my wife Suyoung for never failing to believe that this is the book they're going to make into a movie. Thanks for the faith, honey!

Also thanks to all the ruins I went to myself, in my days as a ruins explorer in Japan. They can't read this of course but I'm pushing my appreciation out over the bonds, so perhaps they'll get the message.

- Michael John Grist

ABOUT THE AUTHOR

Michael John Grist is a British/American writer and ruins photographer who lived in Tokyo, Japan for 11 years, and now lives in London, England.

He writes thrilling science fiction and fantasy novels, and used to explore and photograph abandoned places around the world, such as ruined theme parks, military bases, underground bunkers, and ghost towns. These adventures have drawn millions of visitors to his website michaeljohngrist.com, and often provide inspiration for his fiction.

OTHER WORKS

Last Mayor (complete apocalypse thriller)
1. The Last
2. The Lost
3. The Least
1-3 Box Set 1
4. The Loss
5. The List
6. The Laws
7. The Lash
8. The Lies
9. The Lies

Soul Jacker (complete cyberpunk trilogy)
1. Soul Jacker
2. Soul Breaker
3. Soul Killer

Ignifer Cycle (epic fantasy)
1. The Saint's Rise
2. The Rot's War

Short fiction
Cullsman #9- 9 science fiction stories
Death of East - 9 weird tales

GLOSSARY

Aether – The space beyond the aetheric bridge, where all souls manifest as star-like lights, and lines representing all connections they've ever made with people or places exist.

Aetheric Bridge – The doorway at the center of the Solid Core, beyond which lies the aether. No-one has ever crossed it until Ritry does so.

Aetheric Soul – Another term to describe the aether, though more specifically it refers to all of the souls in aggregate, not the space, and even to the theorized flame from which souls come and to which they return.

Afri-Jarvanese – A language, part African dialect, part Japanese.

Arcloberry – A berry discovered preserved as a seed, deep within the melting Arctic pack ice.

Arctic War – The resource wars for the hydrates under the Arctic ice, in which nations and nation-states cast aside old alliances and made every effort to grab as much ocean as possible. Ritry fought in the Arctic War aboard a subglacic, as a marine.

Arene – The name given to marine who fought in the deserts, hunting for the last reserves of petroleum. They fought in suprarene tanks. Arene is Latin for Sand, hence 'arena.'

Asiatic – A term similar to Asian, but different in that 'Asian' refers to sections of the 'old' world, before sea levels rose and tsunamis leveled whole island nations, while 'Asiatic' refers to the countries and peoples of the new map.

Blood-mic – An internal communication system used by the chord, similar to bone micronodes which capture sound as it transmits through the jaw-bone. Blood-mic captures vibration of sound in the blood, much like sound was transferred to the forming Ritry Goligh in his liquid artificial womb, then relays it to the others.

Bonds – The invisible lines created in space by the passage of human beings. Existence creates bonds, as do thought and emotion. These bonds connect the people who made them to the people, places and things they connected to. Strong emotion, powerful thoughts, powerful action, pain, love, all can create exceptionally powerful bonds. Cutting them, or Lagging them, can create vast power, which can be channeled to exert control over others. They can also be 'surfed,' where their power is used without Lagging, as Ritry does at the godships. These are the resource Mr. Ruin lives off.

Calico – The city Ritry lives outside of, surrounded by a tall tsunami wall. Within the walls life is somewhat utopian, with very little crime or poverty.

Calico Reach – The wealthiest, most exclusive part of Calico, in the hills.

Candlebomb – A type of bomb, like C4.

Chord – A team of 7 marines, each with a name that is one note of a seven-tone scale.

Crull – A genetic cross-breed of sea gulls and crows.

CSF – Cerebro-Spinal fluid, the natural fluid that the brain sits within. Deplete this, for example by drinking a lot of alcohol, and you get a bad headache.

Elba – The island to which Napoleon was banished.

EMR machine – ElectroMagnetic Resonance machine, used by graysmiths to aid in jacking minds. Currently such machines exist as fMRI (functional Magnetic Resonance Imagers) and can be used to take pictures of the brain at work. They don't yet allow writng/rewriting of the mind.

Exos – External suit muscles that augment human power.

Godship – A ship commissioned and boarded during the period of global tsunami while the Arctic War played out, filled with the world's greatest believers. They were all crushed in the tsunami.

Grapnels – Grapnel hooks fired from rifles, with an incoiling function built in.

Soul Jacker – A specialist, like Ritry, who is capable of hacking into another person's mind, and implanting or erasing memories and knowledge. In the Arctic War they served as interrogators, morale officers, briefing and debriefing specialists, skills teachers, and psychologists. Now they primarily work in education, implanting knowledge and massaging it into place. Some, like Ritry, may also erase bad memories. The name comes from the action of extreme forms of hacking, where it seems that the soul itself, or the free will, of a person has been hijacked.

Jack-site – Where a Soul Jacker works, usually equipped with EMR and lots of CSF.

HUD – Heads Up Display, a marine's helmet that can display lots of data on the inner visor-screen.

Engram – What a Soul Jacker injects when imparting new knowledge. It is injected through the eye socket and into the brain as a silvery liquid, containing memories or skills.

Lag, the – The worm-like creature that protects the mind. It seeks to destroy any foreign bodies, including even the inhabitant of that mind, if they come in conscious contact. It can be delayed by giving it thoughts and memories to consume, but it cannot be killed so long as the mind itself is alive.

Lag (v) – Reflecting the erasing action of the Lag, Ritry coins this term to mean erasing memories through the bonds, without resorting to erasing them while jacking in EMR.

Mindbomb – A bomb that functions like an EMP (Electro Magnetic Pulse) for the human mind, stopping all thought and killing any people within range instantly. Soundless and without percussive blast. It can be survived if the mind is shielded within an EMR of some kind.

Molten Core – The exterior part of the brain, most closely related to the gray part, ie the cortex. Embodied during a jack as liquid magma, because it is always in flux.

New Anglais – A new language, a mixture of English and French.

Proto-Calico – The floating raft city that hugs the tsunami wall of Calico, built out of the wreckage of past cities, ships, and anything else. Held up on floating blue barrels, and made up of numerous individual rafts called Skulks. The people who live here have no protection from future tsunami. Their city is essentially ungoverned and lawless, bar the efforts made by Don Zachary to cement his stranglehold over commerce.

QC – Quantum Confusion particles, capable of dissolving regular matter. In this they act a lot like anti-matter, but can be targeted. A QC pistol contains and shoots them.

Rusk, proto-Rusk – Nation-state comprised of remnants of Russian peoples.

Screw, the – The propulsive screw that drives the sublavic ship.

Sino-Rusk – Nation state comprised of partly Russian and partly Chinese nationalities.

Shock-jacks – Stimulants that are stored in sublavic suits, and can be drawn on to negate the effects of shock, pain, and trauma.

Skulks, The – The floating neighborhoods that tile the coast of Calico, making up proto-Calico. They are typically built from flotsam and jetsam, float atop blue barrels, and house the poor, indigent, and those unwilling to live within the order of Calico.

Solid Core – The interior part of the brain, hidden inside the cortex, where no one has ever been before. Here the Lag is stronger, the pathways are myriad and labyrinthine, and somewhere in the center the aetheric bridge is fable to sit. Through this doorway, great power rests. Researchers jacked Ritry for much of his childhood, searching for a way in.

Subglacic – A ship that goes under the ice, used broadly in the Arctic War for stealth and hunting out hydrates.

Sublavic – A ship that goes under lava, used by Ritry's chord of marines to travel through the Molten Core.

Suprarene tank – A giant tank used by arenes who fought in the desert during the war.

Tsunami wall – The wall around Calico, protecting it from giant tsunami brought on by the War and global sea-level change.

Made in the USA
Coppell, TX
03 March 2020